Roses Bloom

In the Ghetto

Shelley "AjeeDaPoet" Fowler

Roses Bloom in the Ghetto

ISBN-13: 978-0692357286
ISBN-10:0692357289

Dedications

Without my heavenly Father, my Daddy this book would
not be possible. I thank you for the gift of writing and the
love of expression.
Sending my love and deepest gratitude to my dear
departed mother, Virginia Medley. I love you Mommy.
I want to thank my children Ashantee Fowler,
for all of her love and support.
My son Jordan Fowler, I love you.
To my grand daughter, Milan Fowler who I love
wholeheartedly and fills my days with the words,
I love you.

This book is also dedicated to all the young girls, young
women, young boys and young men, who are seeking,
searching for someone, something to fill the
voids in their lives.
I want you to know that your lives matter. That you have
a purpose and you are loved.

Last but not lease to all of you that have supported me. I thank all the readers who purchase this book, my first book, those of you that have read any of my work, and those of you that believe in me. I thank you from the depths of my soul. One love!

"Live your life, no matter what others my think or say. A day is gonna come when you will die and people will forget about you. So while you are here make it count. You got one life so hit'em hard, leave you mark on this world and let them know that you were indeed here."
—Shelley Y. Fowler

Table of Contents

Chapter One

The words, "I'm so sorry for your loss" kept ringing in my ears. How can I be sorry for losing someone that I barely knew? Looking at the casket gave me the feeling of being a spectator, with front row seats, to a show to look at a body of someone I knew very little about. The people that were coming up to me all had the same expression of deep sadness in their eyes. The only way that I could convey what they thought I should be feeling was to think of one of the saddest moments in my life; this was not one of them. The tears that I shed had nothing to do with the cold flesh lying in the manmade box. The tears were for me, for all the years of sadness that I endured.

I stared at the body to see if death had done its job, or if the chest would rise and fall again, proving that this whole fiasco was a lie. *Death: one; life: zero.*

"He was a good man, who worked hard to provide for his family. Rest in peace. Heaven is now your home," the reverend said, pulling out a white handkerchief from inside of his robe, wiping the sweat from his brow.

He slowly closed the Bible that he didn't read one scripture out of, walked over to me, then shook my hand before taking a seat. I held the tissue up to my eyes and wiped tears that were no longer there. For some reason, I positioned my hand as to not let the reverend see the smile that came across my face. The thought of this man made my emotions jump from one feeling to the next. I hated it; I hated him.

Please don't let me laugh out loud, I thought to myself.

This was a joke; most of the people here must have known it. Death seemed to give some people amnesia. Causing them to forget how the departed treated people while they were yet still alive. The way this man lived was yet another one of those instances. But for some reason, it seemed to me, in this overrated scenario, they were putting it on thick. How could a man be so good, yet not take care of his children, run out on his common law wives, never looking back. He did not even know if his children were dead or alive, if we had food to eat, clothes to put on our backs, or our emotional statuses. Yet somewhere, without a thought he could lay his head down every night, not missing a wink of sleep. He lived his life like we never even existed. If that was a description of a good man, then give me a bad one. Love and compassion didn't reside in him. The man that was lying in that casket was one of the meanest, most selfish men I have ever known; he was my father. He hadn't shown me any love or affection my entire life, but what he had given me was my first taste of rejection, disappointment, and low self-esteem. My father had set me up on a whirlwind of relationships with men that could see the transparency of my pain. They could smell my brokenness. They hunted for women like me. I was the perfect catch. A wounded soul was my sexiness. It lingered in the air like perfume, staying in a room long after the person wearing it had left. My worth was nothing in his eyes, a piece of crumbled paper, with no use and no meaning. That was me.

I stood up, straightened my dress, and then I proceeded to take the walk toward the casket that seemed far off. I never took my eyes off the corpse that lay in front of me. The sounds of the people's cries got louder the closer I got to the cold, dead body; my father. If they only knew the pain that I had endured due to the lack of fatherhood from this man, those tears would be shed for me. This whole funeral would be to mourn my tragedies, pains, and sufferings.

Continuing on my journey towards him made me remember those times, when I waited for him to come to pick me up. I would wait in the dinginess of our apartment house hallway, pretending that the cracks on the walls were roads, highways, and city streets. My finger would be the car that my father and I road in. We would be taking long trips down the highways, going nowhere. My pointer finger would become raw from tracing all the cracks on the walls to our unknown destinations. Hoping and praying that my father was coming to take me away from here, even if just for a little while, brought a smile to my face. I would stay in that hallway looking at the door, wanting it to open, to reveal my father's face. I wouldn't go back in the house until my mother screamed for me to come inside. I would take a few minutes to move. Slowly, I would walk back toward our apartment door, looking back at the hallway door wanting so desperately for it to open, revealing my father. It never did.

"Lena! Lena! I know you hear me callin' you girl! Get

your black ass in here right now before I break your damn neck! I don't know why you believed his lyin' ass! He always does this to you, and your dumb ass falls for it every time! Hmm, I don't know which one of you is more stupid, you or him! Y'all are both the same, two sorry idiots! Next time you call him, you better ask that bastard for some money! Which I know his black ass ain't got!" My mother would say, taking a long drag off her cigarette, cutting her eyes at me like I had done something wrong.

It wasn't my fault that my father didn't show up. I never understood her reason for being mad at me for wanting to spend time with him. She hated when I asked for him or for my father's phone number to call him. A few times, my mother had told me that there was no need to try to call him because my father was dead. I would cry, wanting to know when and how he died.

"That dirty bastard got shot right in the middle of his dumbass head!" My mother looked at me with a straight face until she could no longer hold her seriousness. Then, she would fall out with laughter at her own lies, and the anger would reappear on her face as she proceeded to say that he had been dead a long time ago to her, so he was dead to me too.

Even though those times were lies about my father's death, the way that my mother had treated me, I knew that she wished he were dead--and me right along with him. My mother would shout at me to get undressed. I would put on my pajamas, lay in my bed, wondering if my father was on a real road trip. Being eight years old, that was the only explanation that I would allow myself to believe. Thinking that my father didn't want to see me would have been too painful.

My mother would call him, cussing him out, not about lying to come to see me, but about money. She would threaten my father by telling him that, if he didn't bring her some cash, she was going to throw me out onto the streets and that he better come and get me. My eyes would light up at the thought of being able to live with my father. I would tiptoe out of my bedroom into the kitchen, grabbing a plastic bag, placing it under my shirt so my mother wouldn't see me with it. If she did, she would ask me what the hell was I doing with it, yell at me to put it back, then call me stupid for getting it. I would place my few little belongings inside, hiding the bag under my bed, just in case my father came to get me. I hope the day would come when my father would knock at the front door, wanting me to live with him. My father and I wouldn't have to wait and listen to my mother cursing and yelling. I would just reach under my bed, grab my bag, along with my father's hand. We would run out the door, never looking back. If I'd had that chance to live with him, I would have in a heartbeat. Her threats never did work; my father never came to rescue me from the nightmare in my life, my mother.

Finally, reaching my destination, I stood there, staring. My hands clung on to the edge of the casket so tightly that they began to sweat, my jaw clenched. Looking deeply into my father's face, my hand shook at the thought of slapping him. Quickly my thoughts changed, realizing that doing so would not do him any harm. He was as dead and cold has he had always been. The only thing missing was breath in his body. He had made me just as dead on the inside as he was now on the outside. Here I am, a grown woman, with that small little girl still living on the inside that wears the scars of wars and battles that I had to fight all of my life. There were no metals of honor for me, nothing, just memories that I wanted to forget.

My two other siblings, whom I knew nothing about nor ever laid eyes on, did not show up. No one had ever told me about them. The only way that I knew that they existed was by the phone conversations that my mother had with her girlfriends, calling them bastard kids, that she couldn't stand them, and that out of the three of us, I was the baby. She would talk about their mothers like they were dogs, not knowing what my father saw in them. My mother would tell her girlfriends that she was the finest thing since sliced bread and that my father would never grace her bed again, ever. She would laugh, bragging about how she knew that he missed her 'good thang,' and that she was taking him to court for child support, wanting to see him sweat about having to pay her more money than he had to spare. If she received any money, I never saw any of it. By the way she dressed me, no one would have thought she got any money either.

My mother was not married to my father and I was not only the baby, but the baby of my father's three bastard children. Even if they were here, someone would have had to introduce me to them and them to me. Hopefully, someone in this totally dysfunctional family had the decency to let them know their father was dead. Maybe they did not need to physically see him, being that he was physically dead to them years ago. As for me, I needed, wanted, and yearned for some type of closure. I wanted to look into the face of the man that left me with a woman that hated me just as much as she hated him. I needed to see that the man who had created me, who was once alive, that was now dead.

I felt a cold touch on the top of my sweaty hand. "He's at peace now," someone whispered next to my ear.

My eyes never left my father's face. All I could see was an outline of a face standing next to me. I knew that it was a woman, by her soft-spoken voice.

Hmm, for all of his lack of love, he gets to rest in peace. He gets to dwell in heaven with the angels, while he made my life a living hell. Well, what about me? The consolation prize that I received was a gaping hole in my heart that I have been trying to fill with men who could never fill it, even if they tried. I thought to myself. I ground my teeth together as I envisioned myself flipping the casket over, hearing the loud thud of my father's body hitting the floor, watching him roll on to the dark gray carpet, exposing his nakedness from the back, hearing the sounds of people screaming in horror at what they had witnessed. Seeing my father's final destination, with his lips touching the tip of my shoe, would bring a smirk to my face. I would stare straight down at him, not moving a muscle, savoring his posture, pleased at his position. The thought gave me a feeling of peace, if only for a moment.

Chapter Two

Walking home from school, my friend Carmen and I made a stop at the corner store before heading home. I didn't have any money; so stealing something was my only option for getting something to eat. On my way out of the store, I bumped into a guy. He introduced himself, his name was Daryl. By the look of him, I could tell that he was older than me, which made him all the more attractive. The way that he looked at me, I knew he could smell it, my emptiness. Even at fourteen, I was way beyond my years. I had no choice but to grow up fast. My body didn't have a choice either. At fourteen, I was already wearing a 40DD bra, rocking a pair of baby-making hips, and sporting an onion booty that could make the strongest of men cry. My body might have said one thing, but my cute baby face said another. Plus, the backpack and the books I was carrying were a dead giveaway that I was a child, even though I thought I was a full-fledged woman.

Daryl was smooth; I had known his kind all too well. He was caramel in complexion, with dreadlocks that rested at the center of his back. He was slim-built, with deep brown eyes, and a crooked smile. At about six-foot-three, he was what my mother would call a, "tall glass of ice water."

"I'm sorry." I said while clutching my books. Giving Daryl the impression that I was innocent.

"A pretty girl like you should never walk with her head down. And sho'nuff should never, ever be sorry for anythang." Daryl looked me up and down and then shot me another crooked smile.

"Whatcha name, princess?" Daryl said, taking a long drag off of his cigarette.

"Lena." I responded while popping on a piece of Juicy Fruit gum.

"Lena Horne!" Daryl laughed, as long streams of smoke came through his nose.

I had seen her in a movie called Stormy Weather on late-night TV once. I was pretty, but far from drop-dead gorgeous like Lena Horne. Daryl knew it, too.

"Hope you learnin' a lot in that school. But you know, I

can teach you some thangs that school don't teach." Daryl rubbed his pointer finger across my science book.

"Oh, really?" I looked down at his finger, then twisted my lips slowly looking back up at him. Little did Daryl know that there might be a few things that I could teach him. This would not be the first time that I mess around with an older guy, and it might not be my last.

Bryant was the first of many that I had slept with. He was twenty-one years old. I met him while sleeping over my friend Tami's house. All the adults had gone out clubbing for the night, leaving Tami and myself in the house alone. Tami's boyfriend came over; his friend Bryant was with him. She introduced me to them. I said hello in my softest tone. Bryant had the biggest brown eyes I have ever seen, and when he smiled, his dimples sunk deep inside his cheeks, making his face look like it had puncture wounds. He had a dark chocolate complexion. His teeth were bright-white with a tiny gap, and his hair was wavy and jet-black. All four of us decided to play cards. My eyes kept looking in Bryant's direction. A few times he caught me looking at him, he smiled. I would quickly lift up my cards to hide my face in embarrassment. After a while, Tami and her boyfriend went downstairs into Tami's basement, leaving

Bryant and myself alone.

I sat on the couch, playing with my fingers, not knowing what to do or to say. Bryant scooted over, sitting right next to me. I nervously rubbed my palms on my thighs. He reached over, kissing me. I had never kissed a guy before. First, it was a slow peck on the lips. Then, Bryant opened his mouth. It was a strange feeling when he put his tongue into my mouth. It was wet and slimy. I opened my mouth and did the same thing that Bryant did. It was like our tongues were in a duel with each other. I didn't know what I was doing, but at that moment I felt like I was on cloud nine. I closed my eyes, enjoying the taste of his juices. We kissed some more and he held me close. It felt so warm in his arms, like that was where I belonged. All I wanted was to be with someone, anyone who would have me. Bryant took my hand, walking me upstairs into Tami's room. He then laid me down on the cold vinyl floor. He lay next to me. He kissed me a few more times before he placed his hands under my skirt. He was touching me in places that I had never been touched before. I did not understand everything that was going on. I felt uncomfortable, then scared. He continued to kiss me as he took my underwear off. Next, I felt pain. Bryant was hurting me. As I tried to move away, he looked deep into my eyes, putting his finger up to my lips, telling me to relax, to trust him, so I did.

Whatever he was doing to me, it was hurting me. Then, the pain became excruciating. It felt like something ripping its way inside of me. Then, I realized that Bryant was putting his penis inside of me. I tried to break free, but I couldn't. Bryant must have known that I was about to scream because he covered my mouth with his hand. My screams became muffled; I started crying. He applied pressure to my mouth with his hand. Then, he quickly grabbed a small pillow off of Tami's bed slamming it down on my mouth so that no one would hear my piercing cries. Bryant's face had gone from sweet and cute to evil and ugly. He never stopped; he pushed my legs open wider with his, forcing himself inside of me. I tried to fight him off of me, but it was a losing battle, so I stopped fighting. I lay there with tears rolling out of my eyes. Once he entered inside of me, there was a burning sensation, like I was on fire. The more he moved in and out of me, the more painful it became. It felt like the room was spinning. I wanted to make it stop, but I didn't know how. Beads of Bryant's sweat were falling down on my face. His eyes were closed while strange noises were coming out of his mouth. I could no longer look into his face, I turned my head, tightly closing my eyes, wishing it was over. When Bryant finally stopped, I felt something warm inside of me. He slightly lifted his body up off of me. I crawled from underneath him, then walked slowly into the bathroom, holding my stomach. Leaning up against the wall, I felt something running down my leg. When I touched my leg, it was wet. I looked at my trembling hand. It was bloody. I knew that I was no longer just an 11-year-old girl, but an 11-year-old woman, or so I thought. It would be years later that I realized that my virginity was taken by force, that I was raped.

That same year, a few weeks after my birthday, I had gotten my period. I did not know what it was. I was awakened in the middle of the night by wetness. I thought that I had peed myself. I jumped up out of my bed. The center of my sheets had a large size circle in blood. Being that I had bled from my vagina when I had sex before, I thought someone had come into my room and had sex with me. I peeked out the door of my bedroom to see no one. I didn't understand why the bleeding didn't stop for so many days all the while never feeling anyone on top of me. I would try to stay up late to see who was coming into my room having sex with me, but I would always fall asleep, never seeing anyone. In my mind I thought that, whoever he was, he was very quiet. While bleeding, I didn't know what to use, so I would use toilet paper, old shirts, anything to catch the blood, so as not to mess up the few clothes I had. I never told my mother about it. I was too scared that she might find out I had sex and beat me, or worse, curse me out. My mother never told me anything about getting my menstruation. Maybe, when that day came, she wanted me to think that I was dying, so that I would come running to her in a panic, telling her I was bleeding to death, so she could get a good laugh out of my reaction. I had to learn what I needed to use from watching a maxi pad commercial on television and from health class. After that, I started stealing my pads from the store every month.

"Yeah, you betta be careful. I just might make you fall in love with me," Daryl said as he played with one of my braids.

I knew what the outcome between Daryl and myself would be. I needed love like a man in the hot desert needed water to drink. Not having it, death was sure to follow. It was something that I could not live without. For me, love and sex were the same thing. I didn't know the difference. Getting affection in any form from a man would briefly fill up the gaping hole in my heart. It would make me feel loved, feel whole, if only for a short a while.

"So, may I have the honor of gettin' ya phone number?" Daryl asked.

I grinned and without hesitation, I pulled out my pen, then wrote my number on the palm of his hand, clicking my pen closed when I was done.

"Cute." Daryl smirked.

Carmen and I started walking away.

"I'm gonna call you tonight." Daryl raised his voice.

I acted like I didn't hear him. I never turned around; I just kept right on walking.

"Girl, he is fine." Carmen smiled, leaning towards me resting her hand on my shoulder.

"Yeah he's alright," I said, devilishly, acting like I was not impressed by Daryl. But I was.

"Well, it you don't want him, then I will take him." Carmen stopped putting her hand on her hip.

"Don't even try it Carmen!" I got close up in Carmen's face.

Carmen put her hands up, her bangles made a clanging sound as they slid down her forearm. "Alright, alright. Girl, you know I was just playing. Besides, we are besties, and you know besties don't get down like that." Carmen twisted up her lips while resting her hand on the side of her neck.

Carmen was a Cuban and black girl. She had dark brown skin, with light brown eyes. She always wore her thick black hair in a ponytail. Although we were in high school, Carmen's body still had'nt developed. She had very little breasts. Sometimes the boys would call her, "Flat-chested Manhattan." Carmen hated it, but never let it show, she was tough enough to handle it. Her favorite saying was, "Never let them see you sweat." Even though she had no curves to her body, she was still really pretty. We lived around the corner from each other. The two of us had been friends since the fifth grade. Her mother was born in Cuba; she spoke English when needed. If Carmen's mother was approached by anyone she did not want to speak to, her English would evaporate into thin air like it never existed. Carmen would say that her mother always did that to bill collectors and Jehovah's Witnesses.

Carmen's father was one of the best looking men that

lived in our neighborhood. He would glide through the city blocks like he was some kind of celebrity. He would speak to all the ladies and give pounds to all the men. He had huge chocolate muscles that he liked to show off in summer, rocking wife beaters, jeans, and construction boots or Jordan's that always looked brand new. He had a missing front tooth, but he still looked good without it, making his look seem all the more thuggish.

I knew more about Carmen's father then I let on to know. Many times I saw him in my house sleeping around with my mother. He would hand me a few dollars to keep my mouth quiet, not just about him sleeping with my mother, but for doing the things to me that he shouldn't have ever done. Whenever my mother saw him giving me money, she would come right behind him, snatching the money from my hands, threatening to kick my ass if I said one word about it. She would tell me what went on in her house better stay in her house, and it did. I was afraid to say anything to my mother about Carmen's father telling me that my body was filling out real nice, while pulling me close to him, feeling my body up and down and kissing me. Or him sneaking into my bedroom, handing me a few twenties and a bag of my favorite candy, to have sex with me when my mother wasn't around, or when she was too high to notice that he had left her bedroom. How he would tell me that I had that 'good good', with every stroke, telling me that he loved me through his deep grunts and moans, and how I felt better than my mother and Carmen's mother put together. I kept it to myself, all inside.

Carmen's father ended up going to prison for selling drugs. We were in the seventh grade, coming from school, the day we saw him get arrested. There were so many cop cars on the street; no other cars could pass on my block. Three cops had him pinned up against a wall. Carmen screamed for the cops to let him go. One of the officers pushed Carmen down to the ground, telling her not to interfere with police business. Carmen jumped up, cursing at the officer. I tried to keep her calm, to avoid her getting into any trouble with them, but she refused to listen to me. The officer that pushed her down hit her in the arm with his billy club. Carmen let out a loud scream, holding on tightly to her arm, as her tears rolled down her face. Her father tried to break free to help her, but the cops started beating him up on the street. My mother stood in the doorway of our apartment in her robe. It was wide open, exposing her see-through black bra and panties, while she watched what was going on. A few men were more focused on her than what the police were doing to Carmen's father. Some of them raised their hands, a sign wanting to know if they could holla at her. I knew that Carmen's father most likely was coming from laying up in my house with my mother. When I looked at her, she plucked her cigarette, rolled her eyes, pushing her robe to the side revealing her buttocks that were exposed in her thong, slamming the door behind her. I could hear a few of the men saying, "Damn!" looking in the direction where my mother was no longer standing. Carmen's father yelled to Carmen that he would soon be home, telling her to let her mother know what was going on. He looked in my direction giving me a wink; my skin crawled. He's still locked up. He would call my mother collect. She would tell him that she didn't do no bids with Negros, unless there was something in it for her. When he had no more contacts to hook my mother up with money or drugs, just like that she cut all ties with him. Never looking back and on to the next one.

When Carmen's father was no longer in the house, Carmen became one of those good girls that had gone bad. She was known for drinking, getting high, and for sleeping around. The boys in the neighborhood labeled her, "the jump off", a name she was proud of. She would always try to get me to date some of the boys around our way, but they were not my type. I liked men; to me they were more mature, more experienced. Then, I didn't know it, but I was trying to use older men to replace the father-figure I didn't have in my life.

"The boys always come back for Carmen. They can't get enough of me!" Carmen touched the side of her face and giggled.

I just stared at her as she snapped her fingers, while twisting what little hips she had from one side to the other, not understanding how she could believe her own lies. Carmen knew the truth, that she was the easiest girl in our neighborhood. That's why all the boys kept coming back to her. She would sleep with them anywhere at anytime. She had no shame. She did it because she didn't think much of herself, just like me, I guess. We were one in the same, just playing different roles, taking it to different levels.

When I got home from school, my mother was in her favorite spot, passed out on the couch, drunk. Her arm was hanging off of the couch; her face was buried in the sofa cushion. I wondered if she was dead. A part of me wished that she was. My mother made a loud snore that could have awakened the dead. That was all the conformation that I needed to know that she was still in the land of the living. I slammed my book bag as hard as I could on the living room floor, hoping it would have startled her out of her sleep, hoping that this might be the day she would ask me what I wanted for dinner. No such luck. She didn't even flinch. Frustrated, I left my book bag right where I dropped it, then walked to the kitchen to see if I could find something to eat.

While walking back towards the kitchen, I imagined the smell of fried chicken, mashed potatoes, corn, and cornbread all waiting to greet me. I would look at the beautiful floral tablecloth where a large glass cake holder rested. Under its dome would be a beautifully decorated chocolate cake. Peeking back, I would look to see if my mother was coming. Quickly, I would quietly lift the dome, swiping my finger across the chocolate frosting to taste it. Slowly removing my finger from my mouth, making sure as not to leave any chocolate behind. I would make my way to the other side of the kitchen. I would open the fridge and smile at how well stocked it was. I would began moving the many items to get to the large pitcher of homemade, ice cold lemonade that was nestled in the back. I would then stick a wooden spoon inside the pitcher, pulling out a lemon wedge, and suck on it. The sweet and sour taste would make me close my eyes, allowing the flavor to linger on my taste buds. Reaching into the cabinet, I would pull out a crystal glass, along with the matching plate. I would hold the glass up to the sunlight beaming through the kitchen window to see a rainbow up close. I would eat and drink until it felt like my stomach was going to explode.

When I reached the doorway of the kitchen, I folded my arms, placing all of my weight on one side of my body. The only thing greeting me was a sink full of dirty dishes, a messy table, and few cockroaches, which my mother called "brothers," that were running off the counter, shattering my dreams of what I longed for the kitchen to withhold. The fridge was almost in the same condition as when I looked in it that morning. The only difference was, it now held a can of Pepsi, a half of a sandwich, and a can of baked beans. Looking at the new items, I knew that one of my mother's male friends had dropped by to pay her a visit of pleasure while I was at school. She rarely got up before 5:00 or 6:00 in the evening. I grabbed the soda, smelled the sandwich, took a bite, then closed the door.

Before walking out of the kitchen, I spotted an unopened bag of barbecue chips on the table. I scooped them up, looking back at the dirty dishes, pretending like they never existed.

Chapter Three

Music had always been my way of escape from my life. I would become one with the rhythms, allowing them to take me away from the harsh realities of my existence. The melodies would vibrate to every part of my body, carrying me away. The lyrics would stick to my mind in the way a fly stuck onto fly ribbon, with no way of being released. Old school music made me wonder how it would have been like living in those times. I would sing like I was a part of each one of those groups. In the privacy of my bedroom, I would grab my hairbrush, pretending I was on stage. My voice would mesmerize my audience; I had them under my control. My fans could not get enough of me. At the end of each song, I would take a bow, waving at the crowd in excitement.

My mother didn't understand why someone as young

as me liked music from back in the day. She would tell me that I was an old soul, like I had been here before. She hated me for that. She would tell me that I was a weirdo, and my voice sounded like a high pitched squeal. I knew that was a lie. My mother was jealous that I could carry a tune, hitting those high notes just as good, or even better, than some of those singing artists. While she, in turn, was tone deaf and couldn't carry a tune to save her life. Sometimes she would bust into my room, cussing me out, telling me to shut up. My mother would take my brush out of my hands, throw it across my bedroom, then slap me in my face for no reason, slamming my bedroom door behind her. Today, she must have been in one of her 'feel oh, so good moods,' high off whatever type of drugs she had cause she allowed me to express myself through song.

While listening to one of my favorite R&B groups, the phone rang. I removed my hairbrush from in front of my mouth, plopping down on my bed, answering the phone.

"Yello. Lena speaking."

"Hello, Lena?" said Daryl.

"Yeah, it's me." My voice was dry, giving off a soft raspy tone.

"Hey princess, you sure sound sexy. How you doin'?

You missin' me already?" Daryl said in a low, baritone voice.

I never responded to missing him. I let that question glide, allowing it to rest in my mind. Truth be told, I did miss him. I wanted to be with him, I needed him.

"I'm good."

"So, you not missin' me huh? That's cool, but I'm missin' you. I wanna be with you, you feel me? Lena, baby, you are more than good, you are fine. When I saw you, I just knew I had to make you mine," Daryl said poetically.

Daryl knew all the right things to say; his kind always did. They knew how to lure young girls like me right into the trap. He had probably done this so many times, that he was a veteran at his craft. Just that quick he had become my weakness, just that quick I could feel him filling up the void.

"So, baby, you wanna see me tomorrow when you get out of school?" Daryl spoke softly.

"I guess so."

"You guess so? Come on princess, you know I want to get to know you, and you wanna get to know me betta, too."

The truth of the matter was that I wanted more than just

to get to know Daryl. I wanted to be his everything.

"I'll see you tomorrow, baby. When you dream tonight, dream of me. Blow me a kiss."

"What?"

"Lena, I know you heard me. You betta stop playin'. Now, blow me a kiss."

"Muah."

"Yeah, Lena, that's what I'm talkin' about. Muah, right back to you baby."

"Bye." I smiled.

"Bye, baby."

After school, I went to meet Daryl by the corner store. When I saw him he was talking to a few guys. When he saw me, he waved his hand for me to come to where he was. I took my time, acting uninterested, as I walked over to him.

"Hey, princess." Daryl said with a straight face.

"Hey." I said, pressing my fingers tips softly up against my chest.

The guys he was with were all looking at me like they were undressing me with their eyes; I felt naked. They each gave Daryl a pound, like I was some kind of prize trophy that Daryl had won, that they approved of.

"Damn! Do she got any sistas?" one of the men asked Daryl, as if I was deaf, unable to hear him as he checked me out from the top of my head all the way down to my flats, licking his lips in delight.

"If I did she wouldn't be interested in the likes of you." I, too, looked him up and down a few times. When I finished I rolled my eyes.

The other guys laughed, but the guy I got smart with did not. He gave me a look like he wanted to hurt me. A feeling of fear came over me. Trying to play it off, I quickly turned my head, looking in another direction.

"Oh you got a smart mouth. I like that. Sweetheart, you have no idea who I am." The guy said in a calm voice.

"Slow down, my man." Daryl cut him a stern look.

"You need to check ya little girl." The man slightly smirked with an evil look in his eyes.

"I'm out." Daryl gave them all a pound. Then, we walked away.

"Let's go to my house." Daryl put his arm around my shoulder. While walking, Daryl waved at a few guys. They shouted him out. He had a look of pride on his face while holding me close to him.

"They diggin' you, you know."

31

"Who?"

"All them dudes shoutin' at me."

"Well, I'm not diggin' them." I rolled my eyes.

"Yeah, that's what I like to hear. So this your last year of high school?"

"No, I have one more year."

"Cool, so you are at least seventeen, right?" Daryl peeked over my shoulder, staring at my behind.

"Yeah, of course I am."

I hated when men asked me my age. It always caused a knot in my stomach. My grandmother once told me that the eyes never lie. That was the last thing that I wanted Daryl to see, so I avoided looking him.

"How old do you think that I am?" Daryl asked.

"Hmm, you look 20, but no more than 22." I twisted the gum that was in my mouth around my pointer finger.

"Yeah, I'm 22. Good guess, princess," Daryl winked.

Looking at Daryl, he looked to be a young man. I knew he was older than me, I was cool with that. His age was not as important as him spending some time with me.

"This is where I live at." Daryl stopped in front a large apartment building.

When we got to his door, I stood there waiting for him to ask me to come inside.

"Come on princess." Daryl grabbed my hand, kissing my cheek.

I smiled at him, letting his door close behind me.

* * *

I had been going to Daryl's house everyday after school for over a month. All we would do was make love, sleep, sometimes even fight. Daryl would get mad if I didn't do what he wanted me to do. When those times came up, he would slap me in my face, letting me know that he was running the show. A part of me became attracted to the rage he portrayed towards me. In the beginning, I thought it made him look strong, in control, and sexy. The way he would get up in my face, making me obey him, made me love him even more. I had found myself thinking that, if Daryl didn't hit me every once in a while, he didn't love me. He was my man, so he could do that, because I was his woman.

* * *

This day, when I got to Daryl's house, all I wanted to do was go to sleep.

"Come on princess, give me some. Then, we can fall asleep."

"Daryl, I'm sleepy." I gently wiggled my body hoping he would let me get some sleep.

"So, you gonna do your baby, like that? Don't make me get upset, Lena. You know what happens when you make me upset."

I wasn't in the mood to make love, but Daryl forced me to. He seemed to enjoy it more when he made me do it. After a while, he became forceful every time he made love to me. I started to become afraid when he would put his hands around my neck, not letting me breathe. I would have to fight him to release me. The enjoyment he got from seeing me squirm made him laugh. Most of the time, I would cry. Daryl would never apologize to me for being so rough. Afterwards, he would kiss me, tell me sweet nothings while holding me real tight making me feel better. It always worked. My love for Daryl made me always go back to his house. Even when he would slap me around, I wanted to make him happy. I had become Daryl's property; in my mind he could do with me as he pleased. He was the only real thing that I had in my life. Daryl's touch, no matter how it came wrapped up, would keep me going. I desired it, but more than that, I needed it.

This day after school I stayed at Daryl's house longer than usual.

"Princess, it's gettin' late. You betta get home."

"What time is it?" I questioned while rubbing my eyes.

"It's after 10:00. You betta make it home before your moms comes out lookin' for you." Daryl smoked his cigarette.

I put my clothes on and grabbed my book bag. I turned around, watching Daryl. He wasn't paying me any attention. I walked over to the doorway of Daryl's bedroom. Slowly I looked back at him.

"Bye." I said

"Bye, baby."

Daryl stayed in his bed, never taking his eyes off his television. He didn't even offer to walk me home.

Upset about Daryl not paying me any attention before I left his house, I decided to save myself some time and take the shortcut though the alleyways home. While walking through the darkness of one of the alleyways, I heard someone behind me. From the sound of the footsteps I could tell that it was a single person. I didn't turn around. I started to walk a little faster, trying to get closer to the brightness of the streetlights. The sound of the footsteps got closer. Whoever it was started to walk faster, like they were trying to catch up with me. I wished that Daryl were here with me to protect me, instead of him being in the comfort of his home watching TV. With my backpack on my back, there was no way I could get to my knife. I wished I had it in my hand, just in case the person following me though the darkened alleyway wanted to cause some trouble. My fast walk turned into a run. Just as I reached the tip of the alleyway, someone grabbed me by my backpack, snatching me back into the darkness. I screamed.

"Hey, shut your got damn mouth up!" a guy said.

"What do you want?" I asked.

"You don't remember me, huh?" he smirked, revealing his pearly whites.

The person that held me slowly walked me up a little to the corner of the alleyway so I could see his face in the dimness of the street light. When I looked closely at his face, I remembered who he was. It was the guy that I had gotten smart with that was hanging out with Daryl.

"Yeah, I remember you." Through my slightly heavy breathing, I tried to act like I was not scared.

"You know, you sure had a lot of mouth the last time I

saw you. You seem a little quiet right now." He twisted a toothpick around in his mouth.

"I ain't quiet, I just don't have nothing to say, that's all."

"Well, I got somethin' to say. You fine and all, but I'm gonna have to teach you a lesson for runnin' your mouth off to me."

"Just let me go!"

"I'm gonna let you go, when I done doin' what I want with you." He got close up into my face.

I could smell alcohol and cigarettes on his breath.

He pulled me back into the dark part of the alleyway, then started feeling up on my body. His hands were all over me. I felt violated once again. I then heard the sound of metal hitting metal as he undid his belt buckle.

"What the hell you think you're doing?"

"I'm going give you somethin' that Daryl ain't given you."

He grabbed me by the back of my jacket, quickly turning my body toward the brick wall with great force. To avoid hitting my face on the bricks, I quickly placed my hands up on the rough wall. His breath was warm on the back of my neck; the more excited he got, the faster his breathing became. I could hear the sound of his zipper. For a quick moment, I panicked. I knew I had to think fast to avoid being raped.

I cleared my throat. "You don't have to do it this way. I wanna see your face. If we gonna do this, let's do it right. You know I was just playing when I got smart with you. I always do that to guys I find sexy. I was mad that I didn't meet you before I met Daryl. You know you would have been my first pick," I smoothly said, hoping he would turn me around so that I could break free from him.

"Oh yeah, you think I'm sexy huh? Well I know you tryin' to play me like I'm stupid. I'm not feelin' that. I'm gonna make sure you never forget me. Naw, ain't nothin' for you to see. Just for you to feel. Besides, this is the position that I need you to be in for what I'm gonna do to you, yeah." He whispered behind my ear.

He kicked my legs apart with such force that the crotch of my pants ripped. Not knowing what had happened, he then took his hand, trying to undo my pants. He fumbled with the buttons. I felt his hand loosen its grip from my back. I quickly turned around, kneeing him with all of my might right in between his legs.

"Oh, damn!" He fell to his knees, I knew that he had to

grab his crotch.

I took off running, never stopping until I reached my house. I waited outside on my steps for a few minutes, so that I could catch my breath. Just in case my mother could see my pants, I took my jacket off, wrapping it around my waist.

I had no idea what type of mood my mother might be in when I walked into the house. With any luck, she might be passed out in a drunken stupor on the couch. Before I could put my key in the door, it flew opened.

"Where the hell you been? What you forgot how to tell time?" My mother screamed.

"I was at the library, what's wrong? Did something happen?" I asked, grabbing on to the strap of my book bag, sliding passed her, avoiding eye contact.

"Yeah somethin' is wrong! This house needs to be cleaned, and I ain't ate nothin' all day! Now get in there and fry up that chicken that's been sittin' in that fridge waitin' on your sorry ass to get home! I don't want your ass at no library this late! Besides, you ain't never gonna be nothin'! So what you goin' to the library for? A dumbass like you got the nerve to be sittin' up in somebody's got damn library!" My mother lit a cigarette, throwing her pack of smokes and her lighter on the messy coffee table. "I know one thing, you betta not be grinnin' up in them boys' faces! You hear me?" My mother pointed her fingers that held her lit cigarette in my direction and rolled her eyes at me.

"Yeah Ma, I heard you." I rolled my eyes up in the air without her seeing my expression.

My mother jumped up, grabbing my face, holding it tight in between her thumb and pointer finger. "Did you hear me Lena? You don't have no time for them boys! All they want is for you to give'em them some!" My mother rested her cigarette in between her lips. She slapped her open hand on her crotch, holding it there for a few seconds.

Being that's what she always wanted from men, I gave her a strange look. My mother didn't care about me hearing her in the act of sex. She would be loud, asking those men to call her name. Some of the names she wanted to be called weren't even hers. She, in turn, would tell them just how she wanted them to do her. Her mouth was nasty. The things that she did with those men were also nasty. There had been times that I would come in the house while she was having sex on the couch. I'd walk in to see men thrusting themselves into her, or her bouncing on top of them grinding up her body. When she was really into it, for a moment she wouldn't even notice that I was in there. Mad that I interrupted her rhythm, she would stop for a brief moment, deeply breathing, yelling at me, telling me to hurry up and get my ass to my room. I would look at the two of them in disgust. Not even waiting for me to leave the room, they'd continue, as I'd slam my bedroom door behind me.

"Hell, that's all your damn, no good, sorry ass father wanted! Then I had your ass! Lena, are you listenin' to me?" My mother blew a puff of smoke in my face.

"Ma, I said I heard you!" I pulled my face from her grasp.

"You ain't got no time for no one! I raised your ass, so now you got to take care of me!" my mother said, plopping her body back down on the couch, pouring herself a drink.

She drank it down, pouring herself another one.

I quickly looked at my mother. She drank down her drink, pouring herself yet another. I wondered how she could even think that she had raised me. She never did anything for me. Everything I got, I had to beg, borrow, or steal. The thought of her saying that she was through with raising a 14-year-old was insanity. *How was I, a*

14-year-old, supposed to take care of a grown woman? kept ringing in my head. My mother's love and nurturing of me should never end. But in my case, it never started. Somewhere between the liquor and the weed, my mother had lost all touch of reality.

I knew, deep down inside, she was jealous of me. She tried everything to get me to quit school, but I refused. I didn't want to be like her, nothing like her. My mother did not have her high school diploma. Her way of covering up her failure for being a high school dropout was to claim that it was just a piece of paper, that it didn't mean anything. I can't ever remember my mother having a job. She lived her life like a vampire; slept all day then partied all night. This was the life that she called a "celebrity lifestyle." But my mother was far from a celebrity. She was the queen of welfare and a hustler on the side. She was just too lazy to clean up, so she appointed me her slave. She would make me pick up behind her nastiness. My mother would leave piles of cigarette butts in her ashtrays, the sink full of dirty dishes, and whatever she would eat, she would leave her garbage around the house for me to clean up. She would leave her dirty underwear anywhere she felt like taking them off then order me to pick them up. I knew that she did it on purpose, to try to get a rise out of me. She would watch me pick them up, staring at me. Her face would hold a tiny grin like she enjoyed every moment of it, hoping I got out-of-line so she could haul off and slap me down. I hated the way she treated me. In turn I hated her for what she wasn't--a mother.

My mother had the ability to manipulate almost anybody. She had the gift of gab that she used every chance she got. If she would have applied herself, my mother would have made one hell of a lawyer. She specialized in getting information out of people in a way I had never seen before. Many times, I had seen my mother befriend people just to find out what she wanted to know about someone or something. When she would get what she wanted, she had no more use for that person. She would cut them out of her life like they never existed. If she wanted to know what was going on, she had her ways of finding out.

My mother was a thin woman. She didn't have much of a shape, just straight up and down. What she lacked in her body, she made up for in her mouth. It was full and voluptuous with words of hate. She never had a good thing to say about anybody. If she did, I never witnessed it in my lifetime. She had caramel-colored skin, with big brown eyes, a small nose that held a tiny gold hoop earring, and big full lips. For some strange reason, the men loved her. Being that she was so mean, I never understood why, until I overheard her talking to one of her so-called friends telling them you got to know how to give a man what they want in order to get what you want. She made it clear to them that she was good at pleasing men, knowing that she would never be without one. She stayed dressed to the max, even down to her matching bras and panties. She wore a weave that hung down to the lower part of her back, making her look like she was a Cherokee Indian. She was the black Pocahontas of the hood. Her nails were super long. They reminded me of claws. All that she needed was a pair of fangs to complete the look of what she really was--a monster.

The next morning, I woke up feeling sick. Knowing that my mother would be home, I got dressed, pretending like I was going to school, but I took a detour to Daryl's house. When I got there, I slept all day.

"Lena! Lena! Wake you ass up! What's wrong with you? Please don't tell me that you got your ass pregnant!" Daryl shouted, shaking me out of my sleep. He was pacing the floor, smoking one cigarette after another.

"No, I mean, I don't think so," I said, feeling confused.

"Oh, hell no!" Daryl stomped his foot on the floor like a child not getting his way.

"What you mad at me for? You act like I got pregnant on my own. If I am, you are the one who did it." I rolled my eyes.

"Who you think you talkin' to like that?" Daryl jumped on the bed, slapping me.

I sat up on the edge of the bed. I started to cry. Daryl showed no emotion, he turned away from me, and lit another cigarette. "Get up Lena. Take this money and go get a test to find out if you are!" Daryl handed me ten dollars.

Before going home, I went to the local drugstore, picking up a pregnancy test. The cashier held the test in her hands. She looked me up and down over top of her bifocal glasses that were sitting on the tip of her big nose. "Can someone check the price on this pregnancy test for me?" The cashier yelled across the store, holding up the test slightly shaking it, before slamming it back down on the counter.

"The price is right there." I quickly pointed at the price on the box.

"Oh, yeah, there it is," the cashier said.

The cashier gave me a smirk. She looked back down at the box, knowing what she had done, she had done it on purpose. I was so embarrassed that I wanted to disappear into thin air. A man behind me cleared his throat while the people standing in the line next to me stared. I could feel all eyes looking at me, like the whole drugstore got quiet, wondering if I, the 14-year-old girl, was pregnant. I felt like a stranger in a strange land. It took the cashier forever to give me my change. When she did, I ran out of the drugstore as fast as I could.

There was no way that I could take that test home with me, so I went to the gas station around the corner from my house. When I opened the bathroom door, the smell of urine hit me in the face. It smelled so strong that it caused my eyes to squint. The toilet was so nasty that I squatted down on the floor to pee on the stick for fear that something might crawl up inside of me. Knowing that I had to find out my fate, I dealt with filthiness and the smell that lingered inside the tiny bathroom. I turned over the box to see if I had the match I was looking for. Two lines; my heart sank. Two lines meant I was no longer alone but with child. I began to vomit out of fear that came wrapped up in the form of my mother. I didn't know if she would throw me out, beat me, beat the baby out of me, or all three. What I did know was that she would call me every name in the book, making me feel worse than I already did.

When I got home, my mother was in her reserved spot on the couch. Looking at the almost empty bottle of liquor tilted on the table with droplets of alcohol falling on to the dingy rug, I knew she wouldn't have heard me walking by.

I went into my bedroom, closed my door behind me, laid on the bed, rested my fists up to mouth, and cried myself to sleep.

Later that evening, I called Daryl, telling him the outcome of my pregnancy test.

"How do I know that it's mine?"

"What! Are you freakin' kidding me? Daryl, you know I have not been with anyone else but you!"

"Lena, you and I both know that you were not a virgin, when I slept with you. Besides, I heard you slept with one of my boys."

"That's a damn lie and you know it!"

"How do I know that?"

"Because I love you, that's why."

"Lena, I got to go."

"Is that all you are going to say?"

"Yeah, Lena, that's all."

Daryl hung up. I held the phone up to my ear for a few seconds, hoping that Daryl was still on the other end, but he was gone.

Chapter Four

The next day at school seemed to drag. In every class I just sat there in a fog. My mind couldn't concentrate on anything but the baby that was growing in my belly. I wondered if it was a boy or girl, who the baby would look like, Daryl or me. I decided that I would hide my pregnancy as long as I could from my mother. The good thing about it was that I wore baggy clothes most of the time so it would be months before my belly would show. By the time my mother would find out, it would be too late to do anything, but allow me to have my baby. I was scared, but I knew I wanted my child, and I wanted to give my baby all the love that I had inside of me.

When school was over, I went by Daryl's house, hoping we could come together about me having his baby. What I wanted was for us to raise our baby as a family. Maybe this would be my opportunity to get out of my mother's house. I knew that Daryl was upset, but once the baby got here, he might have a change of heart, maybe even marry me. I knocked a few times, but he didn't answer. Feeling sad, I turned around, then headed back down the stairs. When I got down to the bottom, Daryl opened the door.

"What, Lena?" Daryl yelled.

I had just seen him yesterday, but he looked like he had not slept in days. His clean shaven face, now held some razor stubble; his eyes were slightly red.

"I need to talk to you," I said in a soft tone.

Daryl stepped aside, not making eye contact with me. I walked back up the stairs and inside his place. I started walking towards Daryl's bedroom.

"We gonna talk right here." Daryl exclaimed as he lifted up his dreads putting them in a knot, Daryl didn't move from the living room.

I stopped in my tracks, turning around. "Alright." I walked back to Daryl.

I tried to kiss him, but he turned his face away from me, not wanting to be bothered.

Before I could get the words out of my mouth to him about our lives together, someone was knocking at the door. Daryl opened it.

"May I come in?" My mother asked, before pulling on her cigarette.

"Ma it's…" my eyes got wide, wondering what she was doing at Daryl's house.

Without waiting for Daryl's permission to enter his place, my mother stepped over the threshold. She put her hand up in my face, letting me know to shut up; I got quiet.

"So you're the guy that knocked my daughter up." My mother looked Daryl up and down. Daryl acted like he didn't know what my mother was talking about.

"Naw, you got the wrong dude."

My mother snickered. "Oh, really?"

"Yea, I don't have no females pregnant."

"I know it's you, Mr. Daryl Green. Your name is Daryl Green isn't it? Lena, go outside and wait for me." Not taking her eyes off Daryl, my mother pointed her long curved nail covered in rhinestones towards the door.

I stepped outside, leaving the door cracked open so I could hear what they were discussing.

"So Daryl, tell me, how old are you?" my mother asked.

"Hmm, I'm eighteen." Daryl grabbed an ashtray. His hand shook.

"You're a damn liar! You may be able to run that game on Lena, but not me. I know you are in you late twenties, maybe early thirties." My mother shifted her eyes in my direction before slowly turning her head back at Daryl, smirking. "I see you like fresh meat, but unfortunately for you that piece of filet mignon out there, umph, that you like so much comes with a hefty price." My mother titled her head. She held her cigarette up to her lips, taking a pull, one of her eyes slightly closed, blocking out the smoke.

Daryl didn't say a word. He tried to look tough, but you could see worry written all over his face.

My mother took a few more steps closer to Daryl, blowing her smoke in his face. "I tell you what. You pay me 6 one hundred crisp bills and I won't have your ass arrested for statutory rape." My mother lifted one eyebrow.

"Six hundred dollars!" Daryl sucked his teeth as he looked at my mother like she was out of her mind.

"I didn't stutter. Matter of fact, since you seem hard of hearin', that's not including the cost of Lena's abortion. Tack on three hundred more Benjamins for that. You got until the end of the week. If you don't pay up, I will have your ass thrown under the jail! I'm not makin' a threat, but a *bona fide* promise!"

The words that my mother spoke were truth. If she wanted to she could have Daryl arrested with one phone call. She knew many cops. She had even slept with a few of them on the force. Sometimes I would see their hats sitting on my mother's coffee table. I would hear the sounds of sex coming from her room. Not wanting to hear it, I would cover my ears, wishing it would go away. My mother got up just a little closer in Daryl's face. This time they were almost eye to eye as she pointed her hand that held her cigarette close enough to him that the tip of her nail touched his cheek.

Daryl held the ashtray in his hand slightly in my mother's direction. My mother looked down at it, then back into Daryl's eyes. Instead of reaching for it, she threw her cigarette down on Daryl's hardwood floor. With a few twist she put it out with the sole of her high heel shoe, sliding the filter from under her foot, across the room. By the look on my mother's face, Daryl knew she meant business. My mother smoothly backed out of the door, never taking her eyes off of Daryl. In disbelief of what had happened, Daryl stood still like a statute, standing there holding the ashtray my mother never used. Before the two of us left, my mother slightly closed Daryl's door,

I saw my friend Carmen coming out of Daryl's bedroom, wearing nothing but a neon green fishnet shirt. When she saw me she froze, covering her mouth with her hands.

"Ain't that your little friend? Trifflin' tramp, both of y'all ain't nothin' but some young ass hoes!" My mother said, shaking her head, before walking down Daryl's steps.

I stood there staring at Carmen with her hands wrapped around her. If looks could have killed, she would have been pushing up daisies right in Daryl's living room. From that day, our friendship was shattered, destroyed.

The next day, after school Carmen came up to me, trying to explain what she was doing at Daryl's house. I didn't answer her. I just kept walking ignoring her, until she touched my arm. I lost it. I started to punch Carmen in her face. She was begging me to stop, but I wouldn't. I threw her to the ground. I continued to punch, slap, and kick her. When Carmen stood up, her clothes were ripped; her face was bloody. There was a crowd around us. When I looked up, Daryl was looking. He rolled his eyes, walking away, never helping either one of us. I saw him standing next to a group of guys pointing in my direction. From the expression on his face, I knew that he told them that Carmen and I were fighting over him. The guys all started to laugh, giving Daryl pounds. I was not just fighting Carmen for sleeping with Daryl. Carmen had disrespected me in the worst way. She had crossed the line, and I had to check her for that.

My mother didn't speak to me for over a week. Honestly, it didn't bother me. It was the first time that I didn't have to hear her calling me everything but a child of God. She never mentioned anything more about me being pregnant. If Daryl did give my mother any money, most likely she spent it all, and decided that she would allow me keep my baby. Even though I felt sick, I still got up to go to school. After getting dressed, I was just about to leave the house, when my mother stood in the living room doorway with folded arms.

"By the way, that little boyfriend that you and that nasty little tramp friend of yours was sharin' is a 32-year-old, dirty ass man!" My mother rolled her eyes. "Umph, I bet his black ass won't cross my path ever again, I'll tell you that. Anyway, on to bigger things. I'm glad to see you are dressed 'cause we got somewhere to go, and it's not to that damn school of yours either!" My mother slowly lifted her body up off the door frame then turned around, walking away.

I just stood in the doorway of my bedroom watching my mother walk away. *Thirty-two? I knew that Daryl was older than me, but I wouldn't have never thought that he was that much older than me.* I slightly shook my head. I couldn't be mad at him for I too had lied to him about my age. It wouldn't take away that I wanted to love him, to be with him. I knew in my heart of hearts that I was just a play thing for him. Now, he's out of my life. I couldn't understand why I thought that being with Daryl would have been different than any other guy I had been with. For some strange reason, I just always hoped that one of them would be the one to really love me, for me. Even though Daryl was sleeping with Carmen, he was still my baby's father, and I loved him. Being that I was going to have Daryl's baby, I would try harder to convince him that we needed to raise our baby together, as a family.

My mother and I left the house and hopped on the bus. We ended up going further downtown. Since she didn't want to tell me where we were going, I thought that she might have scheduled a doctor's appointment for the me and the baby. She was mad, but maybe she had gotten over it. Maybe she was going to do the right thing by me for the first time in her life. I hoped that she would be a good grandmother to my baby and show more love to my baby than she did to me. Or maybe she was going to let me keep the baby so she could get some more money from welfare. Even though my dream was for good to come out of this, I knew that if I my mother was going to let me keep this baby, there was a catch behind it. It would all be to benefit her, not me, and surely not my child.

My mother and I ended up getting off the bus across the street from the projects. We walked down the dirt trail, where grass should have been, but was trampled out. We passed a few buildings and went inside the fifth project, and up six flights of stairs. The hallways were dark, smelling like a mix of liquor and urine. My stomach was doing flips while my mouth got watery. I felt like I was going to throw up. My mother, on the other hand, didn't even try to cover her nose; she just kept walking. We stopped in front of apartment 6D. My mother banged on the door so hard that the echoing of the loud sound made me jump.

"Hey, Mrs. Patty, open up!" My mother continued banging.

The acoustic of her voice filled the hallway.

"Wait a minute, damn it!" Mrs. Patty shouted.

An older woman swiftly opened the door. She looked

like a sweet old lady, but from her expression, I could tell that she didn't take any mess off of anybody. She reminded me of someone that could be a grandmother; who baked cookies, read stories, and took care of all the neighborhood kids. But, if you didn't listen to what she told you, she would give you a whooping you would never forget.

I had experienced a woman like her in my life. It was my grandmother. My mother was dealing with this man that didn't like kids. She wanted to be with him, so she made me pack up my things and quickly made a phone call to my father's mother, sending me away. I was nine years old when my mother sent me to stay down south with her for the summer. Even though my grandmother was mean most times, she taught me the right way on how to cook and clean. She also showed me how to plant and pick fruits and vegetables. I enjoyed the quietness of her home and the sound of crickets at night. When I went to sleep at night, I didn't have to fear that someone would try to get into my bedroom or plug up my ears with toilet paper just in case a roach would try to crawl inside. There was no smell of cigarettes, sex, or weed. There was no loud music, no people sitting around cussing and fighting.

Every morning, there was breakfast on the table, lunch

in the afternoons, and dinners at night. No piles of dirty dishes, messy tables, and unclean floors. No liquor bottles sprawled in different areas of the house or used condoms lying on the bathroom floor. There was always food in the refrigerator and no mice crawling around. There were no half-naked strangers walking around smiling at me, giving me looks like they wanted to have sex with me or forcing me to sleep with them, telling me that they were my long lost uncles.

My grandmother and I would spend a lot of time at church. It seemed like we were at church more than at my grandmother's house. On Sundays, we would leave in the morning and not get back home until late at night. That was the summer that I got baptized. I didn't really know what I was doing. All I wanted was to get inside of what looked like a swimming pool, to cool off from the heat that was trapped in the non-air conditioned church. My grandmother was proud of me; she gave me a big hug, telling me that I was going to heaven.

It was a few days before school was to start when I got back to the city with my mother, back to my nightmare. It was back to the same old mess and madness, except now things were worse than ever. My mother and her new "old man" had broken up the same day I got home. Before leaving my mother, they had a huge fight that left my mother sporting a swollen black-and-blue eye. She tried to make him stay, telling him that she would find somewhere else for me to go. I wondered where was this place she was planning to send me off to? I hope that it was far enough away from her so I would no longer have to lay my eyes on her. But I had already figured out it was a lie. If my mother, indeed, had somewhere to send me, I would have been long gone. The way she was begging him to stay, I knew he must have been giving her a lot of money, drugs, sex or all of thee above. Snatching his arm from her grip, he refused. He looked me up and down as if I had some kind of disease before leaving, slamming the door behind him. The anger that she had towards him came full force in my direction. She had cussed me out, wishing I had never come back. What she did not know was that the feelings she had for me were mutual.

One night, I prayed to God telling Him I was ready to go live with Him in heaven. He never answered me. Leaving me in the hell of my mother's clutches. Even though she was strict, I wanted to go back to live with my grandmother, to leave behind my mother and the concrete jungle of the South Bronx, but she died that same year. My mother knew that I wanted to leave her house. So, out of spitefulness and anger that her man was gone, she didn't let me go to my grandmother's funeral. She told me that, if I shed one tear for her, she would slap the taste out of my mouth.

"Hey, Mrs. Patty," my mother grinned.

Mrs. Patty didn't say a word nor did she crack a smile. I had never met Mrs. Patty before. She must have been some type of friend to my mother. I chuckled to myself at the thought of her being a drug dealer; she looked way too old to be dealing. I had never seen my mother hanging out with any senior citizens. I wondered what they could have had in common. The way my mother acted with her, it was as if she had known her for years, even though they were like day and night. On the inside of Mrs. Patty's house looked like a dollhouse. Everything was neat and tidy. The only thing that didn't fit the ambiance of her place was a shotgun that stood in the corner by her front door. She must have liked flowers because her couches, tablecloths, even her wallpaper, was in floral print. She had a huge white cabinet filled with porcelain dolls. They were all different nationalities, wearing clothing from their cultures. My eyes stayed glued on the dolls. I wanted to touch them. Each one of them were so pretty in their own way. We all walked through a thick, dark green curtain that was hanging up on the doorway, going into a backroom. I found it strange that there was a long table in what looked like should have been a bedroom and weird looking tools I had never seen before. They were all lined up on top of a white towel on a table next to a chair. There were different types of medicine bottles resting on top of a small wooden table in the corner of the room.

"So Robin this your child, huh?"

My mother rolled her eyes, unresponsive.

"She's a pretty little thing. Little girl, I see you're following your mother's footsteps." Mrs. Patty laughed then coughed. It was a dead giveaway that she was a heavy smoker.

My mother tightened up her lips as she rolled her neck, while staring at Mrs. Patty. "My past ain't got nothin' to do with this."

Mrs. Patty shot my mother a serious look. "Like hell it doesn't. This right here is generational." Mrs. Patty pointed her wrinkled finger in my direction.

"Listen, I didn't come here for no preachin'! Especially

from you! Now, you gonna do it or not?"

"You know good and got damn well I'mma do it. I did it for you quite a few times, didn't I?"

Mrs. Patty quickly turned her head back in my direction.

"Get undress from the waist down." Mrs. Patty handed me a white sheet.

Puzzled, I took the sheet. Then, I looked at my mother, hoping she would let me know what was going on.

"Come on Lena, we don't have all day. It's time to get rid of that damn baby." My mother pulled out a stack of money.

"What? No, I don't want to get rid of my baby! Ma, please don't make me do this!" I cried.

My mother bent down slightly, placing her hands on her hips, stomping her high heel on the beige colored concrete floor. "Now, who in the hell you think gonna raise your baby? Huh? It sure ain't gonna be me!" My mother sucked her teeth. "Shoot, I didn't want to take care of you! Plus, I have a life to live and it don't include me being nobody got damn grand mamma! Like I said, get your ass up on that table, now, for I beat that baby out of you!" My mother rolled her neck as she yelled in my face.

My mother counted out a few twenties then handed

them to Mrs. Patty, who lifted up her shirt shoving them down into her big dingy cotton bra.

"Let's go. You're not my only customer, you know?" Mrs. Patty shot an evil look straight in my eyes.

Mrs. Patty said it like she was running a business. In a sense, she was. She was in the business of killing babies, and today she was killing mine. She had no feelings that she was about to take my baby from me. My plans of being with Daryl were shattered. I was stuck in a home that was a prison with my mother as the warden. My vision of Mrs. Patty being a sweet old lady had been voided. I wanted to kick her in the face, run as fast as I could away from her, and my mother. *But where would I go? I have no one to help me. I am only 14 years old; I'm trapped.* I slowly lay down on the cold, hard table, and cried.

"Shut up your damn mouth and drink this!" Mrs. Patty handed me a small plastic cup. Whatever it was that was in it, smelled strong and tasted horrible. Immediately after drinking it, I felt drowsy. I grabbed up the front of my shirt in my fist, lifting it up over my face, and sobbed.

"Chile, if you don't stop that damn cryin'... Open your legs, girl!" Mrs. Patty pushed my legs wide open. I could feel something cold and wet entering inside of me. There was a lot of pressure, so much that it caused me to suck in my stomach and arch my back. Mrs Patty stayed in between my legs for what felt like forever. I could hear what sounded like a vacuum. I could feel the pulling from the suction, *Oh God! My baby is being removed from me!* I wanted to scream, but my mind couldn't connect with my mouth. Anyway, no one would hear me; no one would help me, I just laid there, not understanding why these two grown women had no compassion for me, like I wasn't even there, like I was invisible.

Out of the corner of my eye, I could see the blur of my mother lighting a cigarette. As a tear trickled down my face down into the crevice of my trembling lips, she turned away, stared out of the window, never once looking back at me.

Chapter Five

By the time I had turned seventeen, closer to my eighteenth birthday, I had gotten pregnant nine times, by nine different men. All nine ended up in abortions, not including the four miscarriages that I had. One of my pregnancies was by a man that my mother said was my so-called uncle. His name was Jamir. I was hip to the game that my mother pulled when it came to these men being related to me. It amazed me that every man that was related to me was sleeping with her. Although I was sixteen at the time, he looked like he was closer to my age. My assumption was right, just off by five years. Jamir was tall, light-skinned with pretty, honey-brown eyes. When he smiled, he could light up a room. He wore his hair in cornrows that landed on his shoulders. He was bowlegged, and glided when he walked. His voice was smooth and inviting. Jamir would be walking around the house with his pants slightly hanging down, revealing a portion of his underwear. I would roll my eyes at him every chance I got. He was giving my mother lots of money, drugs, and sex. Not only was he doing her, but eventually he ended up doing me too. We would wait until my mother was sleep or gone. Then, he would take me out to the shed to have sex with me. In the shed, he would wrap my legs around him, giving me all of him. But when we were alone in the confines of my bedroom, he would take me places sexually that I didn't want to come back from. I wanted more. I wanted him to be mine--all mine. A few times, my mother caught us smiling, playing, and joking around, she didn't like it. She would look at me through the slits of her eyes and angrily send me to my room. When I found out that I was pregnant by Jamir he wanted me to have his baby, promising me that he was going to take me away from my crazy home life. I was overjoyed. The night that we were planning on leaving together, I waited up late for him. He never came. From that day up until now, I never saw him again. It was like he vanished into thin air. My mother never spoke about him, and for fear that she would found out I was carrying Jamir's child, neither did I. He was the first, but he wasn't the only one of my mother's so-called boyfriends, that had gotten me pregnant.

Mrs. Patty had gotten so use to seeing me that she had the nerve to tell me that I was her best customer. I never fought or said anything about trying to keep my babies after my first experience with Mrs. Patty. I knew better. Mrs. Patty stopped handing me the white sheets and told me to get them. The sad part was that I knew where she kept them and everything else she used to do abortions. My mother and Mrs. Patty would have ordinary conversations, about people, place and things, like they were old hanging out buddies. They would talk about the soap operas like they knew each and everyone of those people. I would get up on the table, lay back, and look up at the ceiling. Knowing the routine, I would assume the position, not saying a word. A few times I got infections from the dirty tools that Mrs. Patty used to remove my babies. My mother didn't take me to a doctor. She would get antibiotics from people on the streets, throw them to me, telling me to take them.

My body felt worn out, abused, and neglected. I had let myself become a dumping ground, a toilet for those who needed to release themselves. When they were done, they walked off, not caring about me or my feelings, not looking back until they needed to dispose of what they had built up inside of themselves again. My self-esteem was nonexistent. I had no one to love and no one loved me. My life had no meaning; it was worthless.

I wanted to love each one of those men. They pretended to love me but only wanted sex from me. I would fall for their lies. I wanted so desperately for them to be the truth. When they held me, I would hold them just a little tighter. I needed to savor the moments I had with them. In my mind I would imagine that they were my husbands, coming home from their jobs, and missing their wife. In the arms of each one of them, I found a comfort that I didn't want to let go of. As sick as it was, even from the ones that raped me, in my mind, it was them wanting me, needing me. It was still affection that I had longed to received. I didn't understand it. I didn't understand me.

At this point in my life, I hated sex. I just longed to be loved. The rejection of love had always been a part of my life. Even my babies had been rejected, by no fault of their own, with no chance of receiving love. The only warmth of love and affection that my babies were given by me was being inside my womb, but it was quickly removed from them in their deaths. I never got the chance to see if they could fill up the hole in my heart. Maybe I was incapable of giving love. My mother never gave me the chance to find out if I could. Physically my mother had not killed me, but mentally she had stabbed me in my heart, over and over again.

My mother used each one of my pregnancies for her own profitable gain and she was clocking dollars. She blackmailed each one of those men out of their money, not even knowing if the one she was hitting up for the money was really the father of my unborn baby. She would flash sonogram pictures at them along with a smirk. Even my babies that I had lost due to miscarriage, she made sure to collect a profit from their deaths. If they didn't give her what she wanted, she would threaten them with prison time. When she revealed my real age, they all gave her just what she asked for. With the money, she would go on shopping sprees, have loud parties, and buy and consume as much liquor and weed as her body could handle.

One of her wild parties turned my mother into something I had never seen before--a junkie. She had gotten hooked up with this guy named Coren, a white and Chinese guy. He took my mother down the forbidden path of cocaine and heroin. I noticed her sitting off in the corner, her head nodding. It fell back; her face held a slight grin that disappeared, followed by a long trace of a tear that slid down the side of her face. Her lips began to tremble before her head fell forward on to her lap. I had never witnessed my mother's pain, although I knew that somewhere within her she had it. No one could be as hateful as she was without it. My mother started tricking to get money to support her high. Some of those men she brought to the house slash brothel would ask her if they could sleep with me instead. My mother would make me go in the room to have sex with them. I never did, unless they were too strong for me to handle. Then, I would lose the fight and they would get what they wanted. I had to fight the ones I knew I had a chance of beating off of me anyway I could. When they would leave, defeated, she would get mad, slapping me.

"How the hell am I gonna get my fix now?" she would say.

My mother had hit me so many times that I had become immune to it. I would see her rocking and scratching herself when she didn't have the dope. Sometimes, she would be sitting on the floor sweating, shaking, and going off. When she had those days, I would barricade myself in my room for fear she might come in and try to kill me. I would hear her on the other side of the door screaming, yelling, and throwing things. I made sure to keep my room dark, not making a sound, hoping that she might think I wasn't there. There had been times when she tried to get in my room, but she was unable to. The outside of my bedroom door was full of knife marks that held the proof that she wanted to do bodily harm to me. The drug dealers would make my mother crawl, even bark like a dog, to get her get high. I would look out of my bedroom window, seeing her outside on all fours. One time, they made her take off all of her clothes to give them lap dances. They would stand around my mother laughing, even recording her. I would be so mad, but if I said anything, she would slap me if they didn't give her the drugs.

My mother resented that I would be turning 18 in a few months. I knew that, somewhere in her twisted mind, she wanted me to get pregnant a few more times, so she could make a few more dollars before the well ran dry. It was my last year of high school. I had made up my mind to graduate. My mother stopped leaving any money that she made or swindled around the house. I could no longer steal whatever little money from her to get the things I needed for school. She would not give me money to wash

73

the clothes, so I started washing my clothes out by hand. I had no money to eat or for other things. She thought I would have no choice but to quit. Some times, in school I would wait until all the lunch periods were over, sneaking into the cafeteria, looking for some leftover food. One time a lunch aide caught me. Afraid, I started to leave.

"Hey, come over here." She whispered, waving her hand.

She reached under her apron, handing me a slightly rolled down, wrinkled brown paper bag. "Here take this, but don't tell anybody I gave it to you. What's your name?" She asked in a whisper.

"Lena."

"Okay Lena, I'm Mrs. Grace. Anytime you get hungry, come around this time. I might be able to give you something, but I can't promise you nothing." She gave me a small grin.

"Ok, thanks Mrs. Grace."

She quickly walked me out the door. That lunch lady, Mrs. Grace, didn't know it, but she had given me my first taste of true kindness from a stranger. I was very grateful for her. Many times she had filled my empty belly and my heart.

* * *

It was a few weeks before graduation. I didn't have the money to rent my cap and gown. I waited for my mother to get drunk or nod out on the couch so that I could check her purse for some money. She only had a few single one dollar bills, a couple of condoms, and a bag of weed. With no other options, I choose to do the only thing I knew how to do, what I knew how to do best, have sex. But this time, I would take it to another level, and get paid for it by prostituting myself. Just the thought of it made me sick to my stomach. The next morning, I got up early for school. My mother was sleeping. I sneaked into her closet, grabbing a skimpy outfit consisting of a mini skirt, a form fitting top, and her black pumps. I quickly shoved them into my book bag then went to catch the train.

I got to school early. It was pretty empty; not too many students, and hardly any teachers had yet arrived. I headed to the bathroom to change my clothes. When I put on the outfit I had taken from my mother, it showed every curve in my body. I liked the way it clung on to me, showing my thick shape, like a second skin. I turned from side to side and smirked in the mirror at myself. When I heard the first period bell ring, I hurried up, stuffing my other clothes in my backpack. I threw it over my shoulder, running out on my tippy-toes, so I wouldn't be late for class. When I strutted down the hallway, the boys were looking at me like they wanted to eat me. Some of them made noises, others followed me down the hall, trying to holla. The girls gave me evil stares, rolling their eyes, whispering among themselves, looking in my direction. They were use to seeing me dressed in sweatpants and hooded jackets. By all the expressions on their faces, it was conformation that fo sho I looked good. I walked into my first period class and everyone got quiet. Mr. Kerry stopped writing on the chalkboard. I could feel the heat from his eyes watching me as I walked to the back of the class to my desk.

"It's good to see you on time for my class today, Lena." Mr. Kerry winked.

I crossed my legs. Grinning, I stuck the tip of my pen in between my lips, letting out a chuckle. If I wanted to, I could have propositioned Mr. Kerry. He would have easily given into my advances. Not wanting any controversy at school, I decided not to give into his obvious desire to have me.

At lunch time, I went outside to do one of my mother's favorite things--smoke a cigarette. Lighting a cigarette, I slowly eased my eyes down, enjoying the menthol filling my lungs, steadily letting the smoke out, quickly taking another drag.

"Hey you got an extra smoke?" a girl asked.

I raised my eyebrow at the interruption of my smoke filled fantasy. "Yeah, I do." I reached inside my bag, handing her a cigarette.

"Thanks. My name is Jackie. Aren't you in my history class?" Jackie asked, before lighting the cigarette I just gave her.

I tapped my mother's pump on the concrete landing. "I don't know. I don't remember seeing you." I quickly glanced in her direction to see if I, indeed, remembered her.

Looking at her, I tried to recall if I had seen before, nothing about her came to my mind.

Jackie was a heavy-set white girl. Her eyes were on the greenish-gray side. Her hair looked as if someone had hit her in the head with a bag of Skittles. It was dyed all different colors, like the rainbow. She had a lot of pimples on her face that made her look red. Her clothes were big, dark, and baggie.

"Lena right?" Jackie asked, putting her cigarette up to her lips.

"Yeah, listen, I gotta go." I started walking away.

"Okay, see ya." Jackie looked puzzled.

I had become a loner. I didn't like anyone in my business asking me questions. Besides, my home life was an ever turning tornado. It was a life that I did not want to live. I would never invite anyone into my world of turmoil and pain. I never wanted anyone to know all the hell that I was going through on a daily basis. It was easier for me to keep my distance from people. It saved me from having to get hurt, and me in turn, hurting them. People were devious; I trusted no one.

Chapter Six

I stopped at one of the bars across town before going home after school. Curiously, I went inside to see if any men were in there. I walked in, pretending like I had to use the bathroom. Everyone of those men sitting at the bar looked like they could be my grandfather. If I were to bet on that, for sure I would win. All of them at the bar all watched me, including the bartender, who was the youngest one in there. It felt like a million eyes were on me. I didn't like it. One of the men that I walked past gave me a huge toothless grin. Not wanting to laugh in his face, I hurried up towards the sign that said ladies' room. I quickly went in the bathroom, bursting out with laughter, holding my chest trying to catch my breath. Five minutes had passed when I decided to come out of the restroom to leave.

"Miss you need anything, anything at all?" The bartender asked, while wiping out a glass.

"No, I'm fine." I implied slightly looking in his direction.

"I know. I can see that. Listen, if you ever need anything, you know where to find me."

All the men in the bar laughed, but the bartender had a straight face, looking right in my direction, not taking his eyes off of me.

The feeling of awkwardness made me walk a little faster to the door. When I got outside, I took a deep breath, blowing it out, trying to remove the stench of the bar from my lungs. I quickly lit a cigarette.

A tall light-skinned man was walking towards the bar.

"Hello, pretty lady. How are you today?"

"Hello." I said in a low tone as I blew out a long stream of smoke.

"Don't tell me a beautiful young lady like yourself is shy. I don't bite. My name is Gordon. And yours?" He held out his hand, slightly shaking it.

"Lena." I looked down at his hand. Raising mine, I slid it inside of his, gently shaking it.

Gordon gave me a smile that could brighten up the

darkest sky. When I stared at him closely, he kind of looked like a picture of Smokey Robinson, which I'd seen on an album cover that my mother owns. Slowly, I pulled my hand out of his grasp.

"I have to go," I said to Gordon, gently batting my eyes a few times.

"Hold on, Lena," Gordon said, reaching inside his suit jacket.

"Here's my card. Feel free to call me anytime. Will you do that?" Gordon held his business card in-between his pointer and middle fingers.

I never gave him an answer. I took the card, quickly walking off. When I got a few steps from the bar, I turned around to see that Gordon was standing there watching me as I walked away. He smiled, grabbing the brim of his hat, tilting it slightly forward. I don't know why he did that, but I liked the way that it looked.

When I finally got home, my mother was sitting on the couch watching her stories, sipping on what looked like water. But knowing my mother, it was liquor. Her eyes were shiny as glass. She was high.

"Where the hell are you comin' from with my clothes on? I know you don't think that you look betta than me in my damn clothes! You betta not be out there messin' with no more men either! You betta not let me catch your ass out there! What you need to be askin' that school of yours to do is to teach you how to keep your legs closed!" My mother slammed her glass on the coffee table. She pulled on her cigarette, popping her gum, while shaking her leg that was crossed over the other.

Mad at myself for not changing my clothes before I came home, I didn't even bother to answer her. I could see her staring at me when I walked passed her. Her evil look felt like heat on the side of my face. The words that she spoke were full of lies. What she wanted desperately was to catch me with a man, hoping I would get pregnant so she could scam another dude out of his money.

"You betta not even think about askin' me if I cooked 'cause I sure as hell didn't! And take off my got damn clothes!" my mother screamed towards my bedroom.

Instead of my mother's name being Robin Cantrell Johnson, it should have been, Never Always Johnson. My mother acted like she cooked most days; she never cooked, never did any real food shopping, never cleaned the house, and never washed clothes. But she was always smoking, getting high, drinking, laying up with men, and swindling people out of their money. In my room, I locked the door behind me. Throwing my book bag on the bed. I pulled out the bag of food that Mrs. Grace had once again given to me. I plopped down on my bed and ate the turkey sandwich and drank one of the apple juices. I let out a deep sigh then quickly stood up, putting the rest of the non-perishable foods in a Ziploc, hiding it in my closet, safe from my mother and the roaches.

* * *

A few days had passed; I could not stop thinking about Gordon. Hoping to find his card, I searched my book bag. When I found it, I stuck it in the back pocket of my stone-washed jeans. I could not call him from my house. My mother had a habit of picking up the other phone and listening to my conversations. I grabbed my jacket and rushed for the door to walk around the corner to the one of the last standing payphone to give Gordon a call.

"Where the hell you think you goin'?" my mother shouted.

"To the corner store."

"For what, and with what money? Lena! Lena! You betta get your black ass back into this house!" my mother said in a slurred tone that turned into laughter.

I didn't bother to answer her. I slammed the door and left. She was drunk and high. Also, not wanting to miss her stories, I knew that she wouldn't come after me.

On my short journey to the payphone, a few guys tried to holla at me, but my mind wasn't on them. One, they couldn't do anything for me, and two, I was trying to find out about Gordon, who I knew from his appearance that he was well capable of helping me. While dialing Gordon's number, I was thinking of a way to get the money that I needed from him for my cap and gown without having to sleep with him. I would try to sweet talk him out of the money then be done with him. I had to work my way up to asking him, but I didn't have much time to do it. I remember my mother's tactics. She would smile, show a little skin, even sleep with men to get what she wanted. I would hear her say "If they want some of this, they gonna have to pay for it. I ain't given nothin away for free!" Then, she would laugh, that evil laugh of hers.

"Hello?" Gordon sounded like he was sleeping.

"Hey." I didn't say anything else, wondering if he remembered who I was.

"Hey Lena, I'm glad that you called. So, when can I see

that pretty little face again?"

I looked around at my surrounding, rolling my eyes at some random dude all up in my mouth giving me that 'waddup, ma' glare. "How about tomorrow, around 3:30? Meet me by the bar."

"Alright, tomorrow then. Don't stand me up," Gordon laughed.

I didn't laugh with him. I hung up without even saying goodbye. I wanted to see if he would still meet me after hanging up on him. If he did then I knew for sure I could con him out of some of his money.

* * *

The sound of my alarm clock blaring made me roll over. It read 9:00 in the morning, and I was late for school.

"Damn!" I flung my covers off of me.

I jumped up out the bed, taking off my tank top and boy short panties as I ran into the bathroom. I rushed to take a shower then got dressed for school. I peeked into my mother's room, hoping I could grab something from her closet. She was not home. She must have stayed out all night because getting up in the morning was something she didn't do. My mother being out of the house was the perfect opportunity for me to get another outfit out of her closet to meet Gordon after my school day was done. I took my time looking for something super sexy to wear before heading out the door. Being that I was already late and mad that I missed breakfast at school, I would make it my business to go to the corner store to steal my breakfast. I would quickly stick a honey bun and a small container of milk under my shirt, walking out like I didn't want anything.

Today was the worst day at school. I forgot both of my textbooks and my homework on my dresser. On top of all of that, my butt was still sleepy. Before going to bed, I forgot to lock my bedroom door. My mother had appointed herself to come into my room around 4:00 in the morning, looking to start a fight with me. Of course, she was drunk and high as usual. I was not in the mood to argue with her, so I just laid there with my covers over my head while she cussed me out, letting me know whatever evil thing she thought about me. After a while, she shut up when I ignored her, which made her mad. She knocked everything on top of my dresser on to the floor before she stumbled out of my room, slamming the door, still cussing. Not wanting her to come back into my room, I refused to turn on the light to pick up my stuff, just in case she wanted to come back for round two. I heard a car horn blowing. My mother said a few cuss words before slamming the front door behind her.

I couldn't wait for recess so I could have a smoke. Then, I remembered that I didn't have any cigarettes. When I walked outside, I was hoping there was someone I could bum one from. Jackie was standing up against the stone wall. She looked towards my direction. "Hey girl, what's up?" Jackie said standing straight up.

I walked over to her, not that I wanted to be bothered, but I wanted a cigarette.

She held up her hand to give me a pound. I looked down at it, then looked back at her, before turning my head in another direction.

"So, you gonna leave me hanging?" Jackie put her hand down.

"You got a cig?" I asked, watching Jackie take a drag from hers, longing to have one.

"Oh, yeah, besides I owe you one." Jackie opened the box, allowing me to take one.

"How about I take one for now and one for later? Now, I owe you one." I waited for Jackie's response.

"Cool." Jackie placed her pack of cigarettes back in her pocket.

"Listen, there's a party going on tonight, you wanna go?" Jackie asked blowing out her smoke.

"Naw, I'm not into the partying scene." I never looked in her direction.

"Hell, man! Then, what are you into?" Jackie stood back up off the wall, putting one hand on her hip.

"What I'm into is none of your got damn business!" I got up in Jackie's face.

"What's with you, man? I'm just trying to be your friend, that's all." Jackie kicked a pebble that was on the ground.

"Listen, I don't need any friends! So don't be trying to be one to me!" I let out a deep breath. "Thanks for the cigarettes." I turned to walk away.

"What you running from, man?" Jackie looked at me.

I stared deeply into Jackie's eyes. "Myself." I plucked my cigarette, taking another look at Jackie before going back inside the school.

Chapter Seven

Before school let out, I went to change my clothes to meet up with Gordon. I had grabbed a tube of my mother's red lipstick, putting it on my big full lips. Taking a piece of tissue, I paper blotted off the excess. I had no idea why I was doing it. All I knew was I saw a lady in a movie doing it and it looked nice when she finished. I pulled my long braids up into a ponytail on the top of my head, letting them drape down each side on to my shoulders, like Janet Jackson did in Poetic Justice. When I got to the bar, Gordon was not there. A few men passing by were looking at me, not with a look of, 'Hello, how you doing?' but the, 'I want me some of that,' look. I rolled my eyes at each and every one of them. I took out a piece of gum, folding it in half on my tongue.

'*Hmm, maybe Gordon got upset with me, 'cause I hung*

up on him.' I thought to myself as I looked down.

I waited a more few minutes. Just when I was about to leave, someone was blowing their car horn. When I turned around, it was Gordon. He waved his hand for me to come. I hesitated for a few seconds. When I did move, I walked toward him like a model strolling on the runway, slow and steady in my mother's high-wedge heels. I wore a multi-colored, striped, short skirt that exposed my long legs, which glistened in the sun from the Shea Butter that I applied. I also wore a short, black shirt that tilted to one side, showing my shoulder and just a hint of my belly. Gordon's eyes lit up when I walked over to his car. He drove a black BMW Alpina B7. I glided over to the driver side.

"Hey, Lena. You look beautiful." Gordon tilted his body towards his car door.

'Damn, he smells so good.' I slightly eased my eyes down taking it all in.

"Thanks, nice ride." I looked up and down the side of the car.

"You like? It would look even better with you inside. Come on Lena, let me take you for a ride." Gordon smiled. He got out of the driver side, opening up the passenger side door, waiting for me to get in.

I put one foot inside his car then placed my hand up on the top of his car door. "Don't try anything stupid, 'cause I got something for you, if you do," I said, looking Gordon straight in his bold green eyes. I didn't crack a smile.

"Yes, ma'am." Gordon held both his hands up, giving me a crooked grin.

I got in. Gordon closed the door behind me. I watched him as he walked over to the driver side of his car. He was so smooth and cool with his body movements that it caused me not to be able to take my eyes off of him. I did it nonchalantly, not wanting him to notice. It was a shame that I had to play him, but love was not in the cards for me. All I wanted was some money. Then, hopefully I could bounce without giving up my goods.

We drove uptown. Gordon parked in the parking lot of a Dominican restaurant. Once inside, Gordon ordered baked chicken, stewed beef, rice and beans, yucca, plantains, and a salad. I had not seen so much food at one time in my life. It reminded me of the holidays. My mother never did Thanksgiving or Christmas dinners. If it wasn't for the television, I would never have known about people eating big meals on those days. That was my only view of a large variety of foods, of families sitting, laughing, and eating together. My mouth would water from looking at so much food, wishing I had meals like those to eat with families like them.

Gordon served me a plate. I was trying to get as much food in my mouth as I could.

"Slowly down, baby. The food is not going anywhere." Gordon rested his hand on top of mine.

I looked up from my plate. I felt embarrassed. I must have looked like some kind of wild animal eating. I knew nothing about table manners or how to conduct myself in a restaurant. This was my first time ever being inside of one, and it showed. I looked around to see if people were watching me. I wanted to hide. I looked at Gordon. He gave me a non- judgmental look, a look of understanding. I wiped my mouth with the back of my hand. I slowed down chewing the large amount of the meal that I already had in my mouth. Then, slowly I continued to eat my food.

After our huge meal, Gordon took me to the mall. We walked around, shared some ice cream and a few laughs. We went into a jewelry store. I gently rested my hands on the side of the jewelry counter. I was amazed at all the shiny rings, necklaces, bracelets, and earrings. My eyes were mesmerized by all of the bling.

"Lena, sweetheart, let's go." Gordon softly said.

My eyes stayed glued on the jewels.

"Lena."

"Huh?" I looked up at Gordon. He was grinning at me.

"Let's go."

We walked over to a large water fountain in the center of the mall. Gordon and I sat on a bench. For a brief moment, I closed my eyes, taking in the tranquil sounds of the water. Gordon looked deep into my eyes.

"Lena, this is for you." Gordon pulled out a long gold box. He handed it to me. I held it in my hand for a moment, slowly lifting the lid. Inside was a gold bracelet with diamonds all around it.

My eyes widened. "What? Is this for me?" My voice slightly cracked.

"Yes, Lena, it's for you. A beautiful bracelet for a beautiful young lady." Gordon touched my chin.

"I don't know what to say. Nobody has never done nothing like this for me before." I looked down at the bracelet with a look of disbelief.

"Well, it's about time somebody did," Gordon smiled.

The thought of trying to take Gordon for his money

had subsided. In my entire life, no one had ever done anything for me like what Gordon had done. I couldn't understand why a man wanted to do something so nice for me. There had to be a catch. I was curious to know what Gordon had up his sleeve. Maybe he was going to take me to a hotel after this, wanting to have sex with me for repayment. That was something that I didn't want to do. If that's what he was planning, it wasn't going down like that. At least I had a bracelet that I could pawn if he tried anything underhanded.

We left the mall then headed back downtown. I admired the beauty of the lights, along with refreshing coolness of the night air. It was a perfect combination. I quickly glanced over at Gordon. He rested his hand on top of his steering wheel. His posture was sexy. At that moment, I realized that we looked like a good combination.

"Where do you live Lena? I'll take you home." Gordon asked, turning down the music.

I was surprised that he was ready to take me home. It threw me off. Not understanding, I stared at Gordon for a few seconds.

"You can let me out in front of the bar," I said softly.

"No, Lena. It's too dangerous for you to be walking out

here by yourself. I will take you home."

I squinted my eyes. "Alright."

I did not tell Gordon where my real house was. I waited until I saw a halfway decent looking house to have him stop in front of.

"I live right there." I pointed at a home that was a few blocks away from my rundown house.

"Ok, listen, give me a call when you get inside." Gordon pulled over.

"I can't. I don't have a phone." I put my head down knowing I had lied.

"So, where did you call me from before?"

"A payphone."

"Hmm, okay." Gordon nodded his head a few times. "Then, meet me tomorrow same place, same time." Gordon looked over at me.

"Okay, oh, thanks," I said.

Gordon opened up his door. I got out of the car before Gordon had the chance to get out to open his passenger side door. I had seen that move from the movies.

"'Night." I said.

"Goodnight, Lena."

I ran into the driveway, pretending to go inside on the

side of the house. I peeked through the bushes, waiting for Gordon to drive off. When he did, I went home.

Just before getting to my house, I took the bracelet off that Gordon had brought me, placing it in a little compartment of my book bag. If my mother had seen it, she would be asking me a lot of questions about where it came from. I knew that, if she found it, it would come up missing. I ran into the backyard, into the rusty shed, to change out of my mother's clothes, putting my clothes back on. From inside the shed, I could hear loud music playing. The sound let me know that my mother was having one of her "get-togethers." I had to prepare myself for what might be going on inside. I knew it would not be anything that I wanted to endure. All of the happiness that I had with Gordon was about to change into despair.

I hated the people that my mother hung around with. All of them were nothing but a bunch of bums, loving their drama filled lives, living for the next good time. Their occupations were to cause havoc and destruction. They clung to each other like leaches, sucking the very life out of each other. They would laugh, smile, get high, and stab each other in the back. None of them could be trusted. I would see my mother's so-called girlfriends with a man then she would end up with them. I would see my mother in her room with them, stretched out across her bed, smoking, smiling like she was triumphant in having them in her bed. Then, she would turn around, grinning in the faces' of her girlfriends, not caring about what she had done. They were all ruthless, using their energy for evil. When they would speak to me, I would act like they were not there, like they never existed. My mother would yell at me for not acknowledging them, telling me that I was disrespectful. I would stare at her in disgust. It amazed me how she wanted me to be respectful to them when she had no respect for anybody, not even herself. I would cut my eyes at them, never opening my mouth, even if it cost me a slap in the face. I didn't care. I didn't care about them or my mother. I rolled my eyes up to the ceiling of the shed, took a deep breath, then took my short walk and went inside the house.

Chapter Eight

Pushing open the door, I tightened up my face, seeing that there were wall to wall people in my mother's house. They were drinking, smoking weed and crack, sniffing cocaine, a few of them were even shooting dope, dancing, playing cards, and eating. My mother liked to have people over, but this party she was having was over-the-top ridiculous. My suspicions of what I heard were right. She had come into a good amount of money. One of my mother's men dropped by yesterday, giving her envelope stacked with money. I thought that I heard him telling her that she better not spend up all his money, but knowing my mother, she was planning on spending every dime of it and not minding if she got her ass whipped for it. It wouldn't be the first time one of her men beat her for spending up their money. This time would not be the last.

The music was so loud that I could hardly hear myself think. In the living room the blue lights made it hard for me to see the people's faces clearly until they were up close. Some of the men were trying to hit on me, but when they took a look at the expression on my face, they backed off. I had learned to fight off my mother's men. I would not allow them to put their filthy hands on my body or violate me the way they did in the past. I was no longer that little, timid girl, afraid to speak up or fight back. If any of them tried to come and invade my space, they would feel the wrath of Lena.

Wanting to see if someone had brought some wine coolers, I headed towards the kitchen, but was detoured by the sound of my mother's yelling voice.

"Lena, sweetheart, there goes my baby!" My mother held up her glass, letting some of whatever she was drinking splash out on to the carpet.

Hearing my mother call me baby and sweetheart, there was no doubt that she was extremely drunk. When I got closer to her I could see that she was not only drunk but high as a kite. Her eyes looked like she was of Chinese descent. She pulled up her slouching body and grabbed me by my waist, pulling me close to her.

"Ain't she beautiful? My baby is the prettiest girl in the world!" My mother grabbed my face, kissing my cheek.

"Cut it out, Ma. You're drunk!" I pulled away from her.

"Come back here, Lena! Damn it, I said come back!" My mother stumbled over her own feet following me.

"Calm down, Robin!" A guy grabbed my mother's arm.

"If you don't get your filthy hands off of me, I will slice your face wide open and gut you like a fish! Matter of fact, get your black triflin' ass outta of my house!" With a sweat filled face, my mother looked at her arm, then back at the man. He let her go.

"Just for that, don't call me when you wanna get high!" The man walked away from my mother.

My mother laughed. Then, just as quickly as she had done so, her expression faded to black. "I don't need you, punk! Joka's like your sorry ass come a dime a dozen!" My mother threw her glass in the man's direction, hitting the entertainment center. She looked strangely around the living room. Wobbling, she rested her hand on the side of her head. "And turn that got damn music back on!"

When I saw my mother coming towards me, I quickly went into my room, slamming the door, locking it. My mother tried to open it.

"Lena, you betta open this damn door!" my mother banged. She frantically shook the doorknob. "You know what, Lena, you ain't nothin' but a whore! The only thing you ever gonna be good for, is layin' on your back! Your dumbass ain't even smart enough to get paid for it! You just give it away for free! Slut! You cheap, no-good slut! You are worthless, just like your no-good daddy! A worthless whore! He ain't nothin' and neither are you! "

My mother's words cut like a knife. I tightly covered my ears to try to block them out, but they went right through my fingers, entering in, landing on my heart. *How could a woman that gave me life hate me? I wondered, when she first saw me, did she even have any love in her heart for me? Did she ever kiss me or ever hold me close to her? Would she smile at me every time she looked at my tiny face? Did she ever place her nose up against my soft skin, smelling the scent of me? Did she ever place me on her breast to feed me, or did she ever so gently rock me to sleep?*

I imagined my mother showing me off to family and friends when I was born, being so proud that I was her daughter. She would take me to the park, placing me on a swing, smiling at me. I would laugh as she grabbed my tiny, chubby legs each time the swing came near to her. When I would fall, she would run to rescue me from my pain, kissing away my hurt. She would hug me so tight that I would beg for air. She'd giggle, letting me go, then hug me all over again. My mother would tell me bedtime stories, tuck me in my bed, kissing me goodnight. She would protect me from the boogieman that lived under my bed and lay with me until daylight would save me. I was all that she ever wanted, all that she ever needed.

Or maybe she wanted to kill me. Maybe she wanted to place a pillow over my head, letting the life inside of me die, like a candle snuffer covers the flickering of a flame, putting it out. Maybe she desired to leave me in a crowded mall, never returning. I just couldn't understand the level of hate she had for me. Many times I wanted to ask her why, but I felt like I would be showing a sign of weakness on my part. I had to let her see me strong, invincible. My strength was destroying my mother. Thinking that she could not break me angered her. She hated my strength; it was her weakness. I was weak but her not knowing it made me strong. We were two people at war with each other, neither one of us wanting to throw up the white flag of surrender.

The time would soon be here when I would cross over from childhood to womanhood. That was by the government standards, but womanhood was a part of my life a long time ago, just not by the legal standpoint. It forced its way into my life without asking me if I even wanted it. It didn't let me play jump rope, jacks, with dolls, or even hopscotch. It had robbed me of everything that was associated with little girls. It taught me that men were the predator, and I was the prey, being devoured on a quest to find someone, anyone, to love me, by any means necessary.

My time was coming. I would be free from all the hell my mother had caused me. *But would I be totally free? Would I allow my past to suffocate me from living the life that I was meant to live? Would I let the anger of my mother become hereditary in me, having outbursts like a volcano erupting at any given moment? Or would I let drugs and alcohol be my only true friends to soothe away my pain?* I didn't know, but what I did know is that I would fight my demons with all I had inside of me. Finding out was a chance that I had no other choice but to take. Physically being out of my mother's house would be the start to being away from the hellhole of hate I grew up in.

Chapter Nine

I was sitting on the curb, smoking a cigarette, when Gordon pulled up. He parked his car. Getting out, he walked up to me, kneeling down in front of me.

"Lena, why are you sitting here on the curb? Baby, don't you know that you are too beautiful to be sitting on this or any curb?" Gordon took my hand, standing me up. He wrapped his arms around my waist, walking me to his car. He opened the door and I got in. Gordon got in on the driver side. He stared at me for a few seconds before he reached into the backseat of his car, handing me a box wrapped in silver and pink shiny paper, with a large glittery pink bow.

"For you, Lena." Gordon smiled.

"What is this?" I asked curiously.

"You will never know if you don't open it, now will

you?" Gordon turned his body in my direction.

I quickly lifted the lid off the box. Buried deep inside the mounds of pink and purple tissue paper was a cell phone. It was covered in silver and pink stones. On the back, my name was written in pink stones. It was the nicest cell phone I had ever seen. It was the only cell phone I had ever had.

"Thanks Gordon, I really like it." I kept my eyes on the phone, amazed.

"You are very welcome, Lena. Now, you can call me anytime you want."

There had to be a reason why Gordon was giving me these nice gifts. He must have wanted something in return, but he never made a move that was out of line. I found it strange that he didn't even ask me to sleep with him yet. He hadn't even asked me for a kiss. Most of the men I came into contact with would have done far less, letting you know what their intentions were right from the jump. He also never asked me my age; I never asked him his. That was fine for the both of us. We were too busy enjoying the moments we had together, at least I was. Gordon had a sense of style and class that I was not use to. It made me feel uncomfortable at times. I never wanted to come off as immature. I did my best to act like a lady, as much as I knew how to, not acting like the whore my mother always told me I was.

Knowing that I needed money for my cap and gown, I asked Gordon if I could have a few dollars. He took his wallet out, handing me some money without hesitation, with a lot extra to spare. He did not even ask what it was for. I knew that, after my graduation, I still wanted to spend some more time with Gordon. He made me feel special. I needed that in my life. He took my mind away from all the pain that I had to deal with. He gave me a freedom I had never experienced before, and I wanted more of it.

* * *

On the day of my graduation, there was no one their to support me. When they called my name, I took my diploma in silence. Even in the stillness of the auditorium, I still had a sense of pride about being the only one in my family that graduated from high school. I stepped out of the shadows of my family's history. I had become my own person. After the graduation, families and friends were taking pictures, smiling and enjoying the moment of completing high school. There would be no photos of me, except for the few selfies I took in the bathroom. No parties, no balloons, no family outings with loved ones, just memories of me making it--without the chance of making it. My victory celebration was taking off my gown, letting it cascade down on to the gymnasium floor. I walked out of the doors of my high school, with my paper of validation, along with my tassel, in hand. I was free, ending that chapter of my life.

* * *

When I got home, I began to pack my clothes. I had no idea where I was going to go. I had no real money except for the few extra dollars that Gordon had given me and no job. I just knew that I would rather live on the rough streets of the South Bronx then stay another night in my mother's house. While I was packing, I heard the door open, then slam shut.

"Lena, you here?" my mother shouted.

I could here my mother's footsteps coming in my direction. My heart was beating fast. I was wondering what the outcome of me leaving would be. At the tone of her voice, I could tell that she was in rare form. I was not in the mood to deal with one of her drama filled days. I just kept telling myself that I could get through this. No longer would I have to put up with my mother's madness.

"Lena, you back here?" Her voice got closer.

I never answered her, knowing that I had to save every ounce of my energy for what I knew would be a confrontation between my mother and I. When she got to my doorway, she stood there with one hand on her hip, the other side of her body leaning up against the door frame.

"And where the hell are you goin'?" my mother shouted. She looked at me like I was crazy, waiting for me to answer her.

"I'm moving out," I announced, not looking in her direction. I continued to pack my backpack.

"Moving out? Lena, yo' ass is only 17 years old. You ain't got no job and no money. Please, tell me where the hell you are goin'?" My mother busted out laughing.

"Anywhere but here! I'm leaving! I'm sick of this house and these people you always have coming up in here!" I quickly started shoving my clothes into my backpack.

"And what, I'm not sick of you and your stayin'-pregnant behind?" My mother got up in my face.

"My being pregnant made you some good money! So, why you complaining now? What's wrong, Ma? You mad that I'm not pregnant, 'cause you can't blackmail some guy for money? Well, all of that is over. I will be 18 next month! You will never get the chance to use my body again! Ever!" I looked my mother straight in her face.

"Use you? Lena, you were, and will always, be a whore!"

"I'm not a whore, you are! Did you even know that some of your so-called boyfriends had raped me? Did you? Well, they did! Those sorry ass men would come in my room, raping me right under your nose, and some of them got me pregnant!"

My mother raised up her hands. "Wait! Hold up a damn minute! You slept with some of my boyfriends, and on top of that, got pregnant by them? You dirty, no-good, stankin' tramp!"

My mother slapped my face with such force; it felt like a thousand bees had stung my face all at one time. I held my cheek with both hands, looking deeply at my mother with a tear rolling down my face. I felt a wave of anger come over me. I exploded and then screamed with everything I had inside of me.

"I hate you!" I grabbed handfuls of my mother's freshly done weave, throwing her down on the floor. I straddled her body. I began slapping her then, with a closed fist punching her in her face. My mother grabbed me by the throat, digging her long claws into my skin. She broke away from me. Pushing her body back with the heels of her feet, she leaned up against my dresser, wiping the blood off from under her nose. She looked at the blood, then, wide-eyed, she looked over at me.

"You crazy heifer! I'm gonna kick yo' ass for the old and the new!" My mother jumped up, charging at me, knocking into the wall.

She punched me in my face then kicked me in my stomach. I fell to the floor. I grabbed her by her legs then pulled her down to the floor, she hit the back of her head hard. I dug my nails into her face, scratching her. Lifting her head, I banged it on the hard floor.

We ended up in a full-fledge fight. Blow for blow, we fought each other until neither one of us had the strength to throw another punch. Slowly, out of breath, I got up off the floor, grabbing my backpack. With what little strength I had left, I flung one of the straps over my shoulder. I started walking out of what used to be my bedroom. I stopped just over the threshold and turned around. "Yeah, you tried to stop me from graduating from high school.

Well, today I did just that!" I threw the paper that stated I graduated at her. It landed on her face rolling down on to her lap.

She leaned back. "You still ain't never gonna be nothin'!" My mother laughed through her heavy breathing, showing her blood stained teeth while pushing her weave to the side that was still a mess all over her head.

Her face was bloody.

"Just as long as I don't have to be anything like you! You're nothing but a lying, cheating, backstabbing, no good, junkie, whore!"

"You can run, but you can't hide. You are just like me! Just like me!" My mother pushed away some of the hair that fell in front of her face.

"That's where you're wrong, I'm just like me!" I pointed my finger into my chest.

Walking through the dark hallway into the living room, I could hear my mother's loud laughter turn into crying. I stopped for a moment, then opened the front door, closing it behind me. I leaned up against the door; my body shook. I began to cry. I looked around the hallway thinking that, if the walls could talk, they would speak about my pain, my needs, and my desires. To be loved, hoping that someone, anyone would have come through that door to save me. No one ever came. For years, all the fear that I felt stepping into this hallway, before entering into my agony, had finally come to an end. Quickly, I wiped my tears, lit a cigarette, snatched the door open, and walked out into the unknown.

Chapter Ten

I went to a local park. I sat down, trying to figure out my next move. Blood, mixed with my tears, was dripping from my face on to my white shirt. I watched the drops of blood soak deep into my shirt, making wide uneven circles. I didn't have anyone to help me out of this mess that I was in. While sitting on the bench, it started pouring down rain. I watched people scatter, trying to avoid the rain like they were sugar cubes, afraid they might melt from the wetness. Me, I didn't even try to remove myself from it. I sat there allowing it to soak me, drench me, wishing it could cleanse me from my filthy life, making me whole--free. I lifted my head to the sky. The drops of rain stung the cuts on my face when they hit it. Having no other choice, I called Gordon, hoping that he would be able to help me out. I didn't want to depend on him, but he was my only hope. It took him only a few minutes to get to me. He blew his horn; I didn't even turn around. I felt the raindrops on me subside.

"Hey, Lena, baby, you are getting all wet sitting out here in the rain," Gordon smiled, holding a large black umbrella. When he looked at my face his smile quickly changed into a frown. "What happened to your face?" Gordon held my chin.

"It's nothing." I turned away.

"Nothing? Lena, did you look in the mirror at your face?"

"I said it's nothing!" I pushed Gordon's hand from my face.

Gordon gave me a look of sadness.

"Gordon, I. . . I'm sorry."

He stood there not understanding.

"I really need a place to crash for the night. You think you can help me? Maybe put me up in a motel or something?"

"Sure, Lena. Let's get out of the rain and get you cleaned up." Gordon grabbed my hand. With his umbrella, he shielded me even more from the rain, leading me to his car.

I thought that Gordon might take me to one of the

motels by the highway, but he took me to one of the fanciest hotels in the city. He put me up in a beautiful room. It had a couch, large flat screen TV, a refrigerator, and a Jacuzzi bathtub. From the balcony, it had a view of most of the city. He came back with washcloth. Gently, Gordon cleaned the blood off of my face. The look in his eyes was one of pure concern. I could feel that Gordon felt something in his heart for me. As he cleaned my face, with each pat, I felt warmth running inside of me. I looked deep into Gordon's green eyes. He made me feel safe, loved.

"Lena, before I go, what's going on with you?"

"It's a long story, but I don't have no place to live." My eyes filled with tears that eased their way down my face.

"Don't cry, Lena. Look, I want you to get out of those wet clothes, lie down, and get some rest. Don't worry. Everything will work out, it will be just fine. I will see you tomorrow. If you want anything, contact room service. I'll take care of it." Gordon handed me a white, terrycloth robe. Then, he gently rested his hands on my shoulders.

"Can you just stay with me until I fall asleep? I don't want to be alone." My lips quivered.

Gordon slightly grinned. "Sure, alright Lena, I can do that."

I jumped into the shower. Gordon ordered room service for us then we watched movies.

When I woke up in the morning, Gordon was gone. I got up and turned on the TV, ordered myself some breakfast, and jumped in the shower. After I ate my breakfast that consisted of French toast, sausage, scrambled eggs, and orange juice, I laid back down on the most comfortable bed I had ever slept on. My body sunk down into the deep mattress like I was lying on top of quick sand. Before I even realized that I had fallen back to sleep, I was awakened by a knock on the door. I looked through the peephole, it was Gordon standing on the other side. I slowly opened the door.

"Good afternoon. It's time to get up and get dressed. I have something to show you." Gordon smiled, giving me a hug.

We had driven a little further into uptown Manhattan. We pulled into a parking lot of what looked like a high-rise apartment complex. Gordon opened up my door and held my hand as we walked inside through a long glass-encased walkway. Right in the center of the complex, there was a beautiful pond with coy fish in it. We took the elevator up to the 55th floor. Once we got to one of the apartment doors, Gordon pulled out a key, opening it up. We then went inside. The apartment was bright, with a lot of sunlight coming in, it was huge. The sheer, beige linen curtains flowed with every touch from the wind. It had light-colored hardwood floors that were so shiny that they gave off a reflection. The large living room had a huge double-sided fireplace that you could see from the dining room. There was a large, dark-brown leather sectional, shaped like a "C," in a corner, with a matching large leather coffee table, with beautiful Afrocentric paintings on the walls. The dining room was connected to an oversized kitchen that had granite countertops, double-ovens, and a refrigerator with double stainless-steel doors. The bedroom was massive; with a California king size bed with a high-post, carved-wood bed frame; nightstands; and dressers that matched. There was a huge walk-in closet, big enough to be a bedroom, and an en suite bathroom, with another one down the hallway. Both were done in all white and gold marble. There was an enormous office with two larger computer screens that sat on an oversize half-circular desk. Every room had a large flat screen television, even the bathrooms.

"Gordon, I love your place!" I kept looking around in amazement.

Gordon gave me a slight grin. "This is not my place." He walked towards the large living room windows.

"Then whose place is this?" Standing in the distance, I gave Gordon a puzzled look.

Gordon held his hand out for me. I unfolded my arms and glided over to where he was. When I got to the large windows, I rested my hand inside of his. A few times, the flow from the curtains blocked our full view of each other. Gordon stood in front of them. He held my hand open, kissing my palm.

"Lena, this is your place." Gordon placed the keys inside my opened hand.

I looked down at the shiny gold keys then quickly back up at Gordon. "What? Gordon, stop playing! No, for real?" I said in shock.

"Yes, Lena, I'm as real as real can get."

I stood there, not believing this could happen to me. "Oh, Gordon, thank you! Thank you so much!" I wrapped my arms around Gordon's neck, bursting into tears.

"You are very welcome." Gordon held my waist.

When the reality had set in that this was my place, I quickly ran into the bedroom, throwing myself onto the bed, screaming. Gordon stood in the bedroom doorway with his arms folded, amused at my excitement.

Chapter Eleven

Gordon had shown me so many things. Sometimes I would feel ashamed that I didn't know much of anything, but he loved educating me. He took the time to teach me how to dress, how to set a table, even proper table manners. My mother never took the time to teach me anything positive. Everything that I knew, I had learned from someone else. We would go to art galleries, plays, and museums. One time he took me to see an opera. Gordon taught me how to drive, even buying me a new car. He introduced me to a whole new world; I loved everything about it. We had spent so much time together that this was the first time I was truly in love. But, amongst all this happiness, I was scared. Gordon made it so easy for me to love him. He never forced himself on me. The only thing that he wanted to do was to make me happy;

he always did that. I wasn't used to any of the treatment that I had receive from Gordon. Love was something that never loved me back. I wanted to do the same for him, but all I had to give him was me, which wasn't much. I was damaged goods.

"Is everything okay?" Gordon asked, giving me a warm small smile.

"Yes, everything is better than okay." I grabbed Gordon's hand. I put my hand on his face, kissing him. "You know that I am in love with you right?" I said, resting my head on Gordon's chest.

"Lena, baby, I love you more that the air that I breath."

We held each other in a tight embrace, kissing like long lost lovers. We made love to each other all through the night. Gordon was the epitome of love. He touched me in places I didn't know existed. I could feel his passion permeating every inch of my body. I was intoxicated in the intimacy of him. Our night of love caused us sleep all morning. When we woke up, we took a bubble bath together. In the tub, I laid my head on Gordon's chest.

"Lena, you know I never asked you when is your birthday."

I slightly closed my eyes, letting out a deep sigh. For a moment I hesitated. "My birthday was last week."

"Why didn't you tell me?" Gordon asked confused.

I turned my head slightly to the side, waving my hand through the bubbles. "Because I just turned 18, that's why." I tightened my lips and got out of the tub, grabbing my towel.

"Eighteen? Lena, you look and act so much older than you are."

"That's because I had to. I had a father that knew very little about me and a mother who never loved me. What choice did I have? That's the only way I knew how to survive!" I quickly walked out of the bathroom. Gordon jumped out of the tub, wrapping his muscular wet arms around me.

"Lena, Lena! I just had no idea, that's all. Hopefully you won't mind loving a 40-year-old man like me, huh."

"Gordon, your age does not matter to me. You matter to me."

Gordon lifted my head, looking deep into my eyes. "Whatever you didn't get in your life before we met, I'm going to try my hardest to give it to you. I can't take away your past, but I can damn sure brighten your future." Gordon cupped my face in his hands, slowly kissing me.

I could see that Gordon meant every word that he said. He picked me up, laying me down on the bed. He gave me a hot oil massage that relaxed every muscle in my body. I eased me eyes down as a smile graced my face. Gordon's touch made me feel like I was his everything.

* * *

Gordon had taken me on quite a few vacations, but out of them all, Hawaii was my favorite place. He had taken me there for my 19th birthday. We had spent three weeks there. I never wanted to leave. Everything about it was paradise. When we got back from Hawaii, Gordon and I decided to live together. After getting Gordon's things put away, we had a romantic dinner on the floor in front of the fireplace.

"I'll be right back." Gordon got up heading toward our bedroom. I watched the glow from the fire glisten on his well-toned, naked body.

When he came back, he stood behind me. I felt something cold on my neck. Slowly, I reached my hand up, touching it.

"Happy birthday, Lena."

When I looked down, Gordon had placed a diamond and ruby necklace on my neck.

"Thank you Gordon, oh my goodness, it's beautiful!" I

stood up kissing his lips.

"Not as beautiful as you."

Gordon slowly lifted my legs, wrapping them around him. Slowly, he eased our bodies down on to the crimson, plush blanket. He gently eased himself inside of me. My body surrendered. Gordon opened my legs wide. I let them fall to the side. With every thrust of him, he looked deeply into my eyes. There was pain in the pleasure of Gordon's injections within me. He gave me every inch of his well-endowed manhood. I quivered with every rotation of my hips. We became hotter than the blaze of fire next to us. We fully unleashed our animal magnetism that was within us. I mounted myself on top of Gordon, focusing on every gyration of my body. Gordon held on to my waist, squeezed my buttocks, letting his head fall back slightly. Wanting to explode, giving me all of himself, Gordon flipped me over, penetrating deep within me. Handfuls of the blanket filled the palms of my hands as my head buried in its softness. Perspiration filled our pores. We erupted, letting our juices flow free.

We continued to make love in front of the fireplace until its fire and the fire inside of us had dissipated.

* * *

In the morning, I was awakened by the smell of bacon. When I got up, I peeked in the kitchen to witness Gordon singing, dancing, and cooking.

"Talkin' about my girl." Gordon sang, snapping his fingers.

He did a slide, then a two step move. He leaned back, then quickly grabbed the side of his back feeling some pain. I covered my mouth so he wouldn't hear me laughing. I quietly tiptoed back to the bedroom.

"Lena, oh, Lena!" Gordon sang while walking down the hallway, coming towards the bedroom.

I jumped in the bed, pretending to be asleep.

"Lena, oh Lena, you made my dreams come true," Gordon sang loudly.

Peeking through one eye, I could see him carrying a tray.

"Lena, Lena, baby?" Gordon whispered near my ear. He kissed my cheek as I laid there pretending to be asleep. I stretched my arms, sliding up, giving him a smile.

"Breakfast time." Gordon placed a tray across my legs. He had made me bacon, eggs, pancakes, and orange juice. He also placed one long-stemmed rose on the tray.

"Good morning, baby. Come and eat with me." I patted

my hand on Gordon's side of the bed.

He smiled, then proceeded to crawl to me, so slowly, like a tiger ready to devour his prey. I laughed. We fed each other breakfast in bed. After we ate, I placed the tray on the floor, grabbing the rose. I stuck it in between my teeth, stood up, and danced on the bed, snapping my fingers. Gordon laughed.

"Bravo! Bravo!" Gordon clapped. He pulled me down to him, easing the rose from my mouth. "You make me feel so alive." Gordon kissed my cheek.

"I don't have nothing to give you, but you are welcome to have me--all of me."

"Baby, that's all I need."

"Thank you so much, Gordon, for loving me."

"Lena, baby, the pleasure is all mine"

Gordon came close to me. He puckered up his lips. I did the same. When he got close enough, I licked his forehead. We both fell out in laughter.

Chapter Twelve

Gordon and I had been living together for almost a year. Being that it was few days from our living together one year anniversary, I wanted to make him a surprise dinner. I got up from my nap, got dressed, then headed to the supermarket to pick up the things that I needed. Waiting in the checkout line, I forgot that we had run out of body wash. When I got to the aisle where the body wash was, I saw my mother placing soap that she was stealing in her bag. I backed up for a moment. My eyes shifted from one side to the other, wondering what she was doing in Manhattan. My first thought was to run away, but I decided to face my fear of her head-on. I pulled down my blazer, cleared my throat, patted the side of my hair, then stepped out, holding my head up. My mother looked horrible. Her weave had seen better days;

it was matted, old, and looked dirty. Her eyes were puffy and red. Her beloved fingernails were missing on some of her fingers, and I could see the visible track marks from shooting heroin on her arms.

"Well, well, well, if it ain't my ungrateful, so-called daughter!" My mother placed her hand on her invisible hip.

"Hey, Ma." I didn't make eye contact with her.

"Hey Ma, my ass! Where the hell you been hidin' at? Looks like you been doin' your thang!" She popped her chewing gum, staring me up and down.

"I've been alright. What about you?" I said, trying to focus on which body wash to buy.

Once again, I could feel the heat on my face from my mother's rage. "Like you really care how I've been doin'! How the hell you think I been doin'? You can see what the hell I'm doin'! I'm tryin' to survive and stay alive!" My mother opened up her oversized bag towards me, showing me a bag full of stolen items.

People who were in the same aisle as us left. Other people who were walking pass were staring.

"Listen, I did not come in here for this! Stop making a scene! You're making a fool of yourself!" I whispered between my tightened lips. With a tight face, I looked her straight in her eyes.

"Oh, so now I'm a fool!" My mother slammed the body wash in her hand down on the shelf. She folded her arms while rolling her neck. "You know what Lena, you are right, I was a fool! I was a fool to keep takin' your nasty ass to get all them abortions! Or maybe I was a bigger fool for lettin' your hot behind make my men get out of my bed and go to yours, sleepin' with you! I was a bigger fool for not abortin' your ass when I had the chance! You know what, Lena? When you was a baby I put a loaded gun in your mouth. I was gonna kill you, but your no-good, sorry ass daddy was beggin' and cryin' for me not to! I should have pulled the trigger and blew your brains out and his!" My mother got in my face.

I pushed her away. I wanted to wrap my hands around her neck to choke her to death. I wanted her hateful words to end, to stop haunting me, to stop hurting me. I wanted the lies to stop, for them to no longer be able to torture me, to set me free from them and her. I balled up my fists so tight that my nails were stabbing me in my palms. I wanted to punch her in the face. Then, I thought about how good my life was, how I had a man that loved the very ground that I walked on, and how I loved him with everything that I had inside of me, every part of me. How my life was coming full circle, this time with peace, joy, and love that had finally made its way into my life, finding me. All those thoughts made me unloosen my fists.

"You're not even worth it. I know you want me to stoop down to your level, but I'm not going to. You and I both know the truth." I turned away from my mother. I began walking out of the supermarket.

My mother laughed her evil laugh. "What truth? That you're a nasty cow? I wish I never had you!"

I stopped, turning around, looking my mother straight into her eyes. "That's not true; you wish you were me. You wish that you had the courage to make something out of your life, but you didn't. You threw your life away and now you want to blame me for your shortcomings. You're a failure. I found something that you could never give me, and that's love."

"Love, huh?" My mother let the sides of her mouth fall down. "Don't nobody loves you, Lena! They only love what you have right there in between your legs!" My mother pointed towards my vagina.

"That's what your definition of love is, because no ever

loved you. Hell, you never even loved yourself!" I sightly shook my head.

My mother followed me outside. When she saw me stop in front of my car, she started screaming. "A new car, huh? Tell me how many men did you sleep with to get that car? You whore, you got damn whore!" My mother was coming towards my car. I quickly jumped in. She ran up to the driver side window, pressing her face up against it.

While starting my car, I stared at her like she was out of her mind.

"You no good, whore! I hope you crash and die! You hear me! Die, die, die!" with a deranged expression on her face, my mother banged on my window.

I backed my car out. She fell on the ground then jumped back up. When I pulled off, she threw her purse at my car. A bottle of thick liquid splatted onto my back window. I looked through the rearview window to see her standing there in the parking lot, the woman who was my mother, looking and acting like a manic.

When Gordon came home, I was sitting in the bedroom in the dark.

"Lena, Lena, honey where are you?" Gordon called out to me. The tapping sound of his shoes stopped when he got to the bedroom doorway. "Lena, I know you are in here. I can see the fire from your cigarette." Gordon laughed like I was trying to play one of the many tricks that I would play on him.

He turned on the lights. I was sitting there with my black mascara running down my face. My hand shook as I took a pull off of my cigarette.

"Lena, what happened? Please, tell me why you are sitting here in the dark. And why are you crying?" Gordon asked, handing me a dozen of roses, placing a box of Godiva, my favorite chocolates, next to me on the bed.

"I ran into my mother today." I whispered as I placed the flowers up to my nose before sitting them down on the nightstand.

"Oh, Lena, how is she?" Gordon knelt down in between my legs, resting his hands on my thighs.

"She was the same mean and hateful woman she has always been." For a brief moment I looked up to the ceiling. "God, how can a mother hate their child so much? I never did anything to her. I didn't have a choice to be born. All I ever wanted was for her to love me. Was that too much for a child to ask? Damn her! To hell with her!" I broke down, placing my head down onto the pillows, sobbing.

Everything that I had been through poured out of me. I was unable to control my feelings. Gordon laid me down on the bed, comforting me through it. He held me tightly, reassuring me that he had my best interest at heart. The more I cried, it felt like I was cleansing my heart from all the pain that I received from my mother, my father, the rapes, the loss of my children, everything. I cried until I had fallen asleep in Gordon's arms.

* * *

When I woke up, Gordon was asleep right by my side. I didn't say a word, I just watched him sleeping. His face looked so peaceful, full of contentment. The more I stared at him, the more I loved him. He was my world, my hero, my everything. Gordon had come into my life, making everything right. He gave me new beginnings and a hope for a brighter tomorrow. There was no way I could repay him for all that he had done for me, not just financially, but emotionally, spiritually and physically. He gave me it all. I moved Gordon's hand slowly as not to wake him up.

"Hey baby, come lay back down," Gordon said, holding my hand.

"Okay." I slowly lowered my body back down on the bed, resting my head on to Gordon's chest.

"Lena, I want you to know that everything is going to be alright. You can't change your mother, but you can always change how you feel about her."

"Gordon, you just don't understand what I have been through with her. She never loved me."

Gordon opened his eyes slightly, placing one of his hands behind his head. "Lena, my life was hard, too. My father would beat my brothers and I until we almost passed out. He would tell us that was the only way we would grow up to be men, that real men don't cry. I know about coming up on the rough side of the mountain. I just knew I would never grow up to be like him and I didn't. Don't let your mother win. You fight with everything you got to not be like her, understand?"

"Yeah, I understand." My hand gently caressed Gordon's stomach.

"I love you, baby."

"I love you, too, Gordon." I kissed the deep cleft on his chin.

"Will you go out on a date with me?" Gordon poked out his bottom lip.

"What are you talking about?" I smirked.

"Let's get out of the house and go to dinner and see a movie."

"I don't know, Gordon."

"Come on, baby. It will do you good to get out and clear your mind. Besides, I haven't been on a date in a long time," Gordon frowned.

"Yeah, that's true."

"So, I can get that date with the most beautiful girl in the world?"

"Yes, you can." I slightly tilted my head to the side.

"I love you." Gordon pushed my hair behind my ear.

" I love you more, baby."

Gordon kissed the top of my forehead, then ran his thumb across my high cheekbone before kissing me with passion.

Chapter Thirteen

When I got up in the morning, I decided to cook Gordon his favorite breakfast. I made him an omelet with peppers, onions, red potatoes, sharp cheddar cheese, whole wheat toast, and orange juice.

"Mmm, something smells good in here," Gordon said, wrapping his arms around my waist.

"Good morning, baby," I said flipping Gordon's omelet.

"Good morning." Gordon kissed the back of my neck then gently ran his tongue down my neck causing a shiver to run down my spine.

Gordon sat down at the table, waiting anxiously for his breakfast. I sat his plate in front of him. He rubbed his hands together. "Looks good baby, thank you."

I turned around before heading back to the stove top. "You're welcome."

"Lena, you need a break and so do I. Let's go on a vacation." Gordon lifted up his glass of orange juice.

"That would be so nice baby. Where would we go?" I asked, sliding in the kitchen chair, easing up my coffee mug.

"Anywhere you want to go, babe." Gordon winked before putting a piece of his omelet in his mouth.

"How about Australia!" I quickly placed my mug down on the table, clasping my hands together, intertwining my fingers.

"You got it. Go online today and book the flight. Hmm, I got to make a run baby. I will see you later." Gordon glanced down at his Rolex, he drank the rest of his orange juice before wiping his mouth with his napkin, then gave me a gentle kiss on my lips.

"Wait," I said. I stood up giving him a long sensual kiss.

"Hmm, I like that." Gordon held me tight, jerking my body closer to him a few times.

"I love it, and I love you, too." I wrapped my arms around his neck.

"I love you, too, baby."

"I tell you what, when we back from Australia, let's

make this thing we have official."

"You mean it?" my face lit up with delight.

"Yes, baby, I mean it."

"Oh, Gordon! I'll be the best wife you could ever ask for! I promise!" I wrapped my arms tightly around Gordon's neck.

"I know, baby. I'll be the only husband you will every need."

"I know that's right." I walked Gordon over to the door. We looked deeply into each other's eyes then shared a long sensual tongue kiss. It went right through me.

"I have to go before I won't."

I adjusted Gordon's tie. "Hmm, I wouldn't mind," I smirked.

I stood in the doorway watching what would be my future husband smoothly walk down the walkway. Slowly, I closed the door. I jumped up and down. My body shook excitedly about the thought of becoming Mrs. Lena Lenox.

After cleaning up, I got on the computer, overjoyed, as I booked our flight and hotel reservations. Being that it was Sunday, I decided that we should leave on Saturday, giving me plenty of time to pack our suitcases and to also take care of some household business. In the afternoon,

I got myself together and went to the mall to do some shopping for Gordon and myself for our vacation. By the time I had finished shopping, it was close to 5:00 in the evening. I realized that I hadn't heard from Gordon since he left the house in the morning. Normally, he would have called to check to see if everything was alright with me. Knowing that Gordon would soon be coming home, I went to the gourmet grocery to pick up something for dinner. When I got home, I gave Gordon a call. His phone went directly to his voicemail.

"Hey baby, give me a call when you get this message. I love you. Later."

I took all of our new clothes out of the bags hanging them up in the hallway closet to take them to the cleaners in the morning. Then I started dinner. After dinner was done, I wanted to eat with Gordon so I waited, and went to our bedroom to lay across the bed. It was around 7:00 and still no sign of Gordon.

* * *

Bang, bang, bang!

I was awakened out of my sleep by the loud knocking on the door. I quickly glanced over at the clock on the wall. It was 1:00 in the morning. I rubbed my hands over my face. I reached my hand over on Gordon's side of the bed to wake him up. He was not there. I got up quickly, and went to the door. When I looked through the peephole two officers were standing there. I never trusted cops; in my neighborhood they were crooked, not looking out for the people, but for themselves. I would see them doing business with drug dealers, even buying drugs. I would see some of them getting high with my mother in my house. Their corruption was hidden behind their badges. They were no better than any other criminal. In my eyes, they were the worst kind. I waited a few minutes before answering, not knowing why they were here and what they could have wanted.

"Yeah, can I help you?" I said through the door.

"Yes, miss. We are looking for a Lena Johnson."

My eyes shifted from one side to the other. *Why would cops be looking for me? I hadn't done anything, and how did they know that I lived here?* My mind began to race, not knowing if I should tell them who I was.

"What for?"

"Miss, she's not in any type of trouble, we just need to speak to her."

I hesitated for a moment. "I'm Lena Johnson. What do you want to speak to me about?"

"Miss we would like you to open up the door, so we can talk to you."

I picked up the large carved stick that Gordon bought on our trip to South Africa, placing it by the side of my leg. I put the chain on the door before opening it slightly.

"Let me see your badges," I said, peeking through the small opening in the door.

Both officers showed me their badges. I looked at them closely. Then, I removed the chain, opening the door a little wider.

"Sorry to disturb you, miss, but there has been an accident." Both officers took off their hats.

"What are you taking about?" My eyes shifted between both of the officers.

"Do you know a Gordon Lenox?" one of the officers asked.

"Why? Did he do something wrong?" I said, hoping everything was alright.

"No ma'am. Please let us know if you know him."

"Yes, I do. Was he hurt?"

"Ma'am, he…"

"He's in the hospital? Oh my God! What hospital is he in?"

"Ma'am," the other officer said.

I ran into the kitchen to get my car keys and my purse then headed back to the door where the officers were standing.

"Please, tell me what hospital he is in!" I held my keys tightly in my hand.

Both officers looked at each other.

"Are you just going to stand there? For God's sake tell me where he is!"

One officer nodded at the other. "Miss, Gordon is dead. He was killed in a shoot out over on Madison Boulevard. He was driving when a stray bullet entered his car. I'm sorry," one of the officers said, rubbing the brim of his hat.

For a moment, I stared at the officers like they were speaking a foreign language. "This must be some kind of joke! Not my Gordon!" I dropped my purse and my car keys.

"No, no, please tell me this is a mistake!"

"I'm sorry miss," the other officer said.

"Not my Gordon! Gordon! Oh, Gordon!" I screamed. My body too weak to hold up I fell on to the floor. It felt like everything around me was moving in slow motion. "Gordon, please come home! Gordon, please don't leave me please! Oh, God, please, please!" The officers helped me up, sitting me down the couch.

"Miss, is there anyone you would like us to call to come and be with you?"

"I have no one, no one! He was the only somebody that I had! I don't have nobody else!" I burst into tears, shaking my head, not understanding.

"Miss, if you need anything, be sure to call us." The two offices left.

I sat in shock and disbelief that the man that I had loved with all of my heart was now dead. The life that I knew was gone in an instant. Once again, love had been ripped from me, taken away without my permission, leaving yet a bigger hole in my heart. What was I going to do without Gordon in my life? He was the only somebody who had shown me the true meaning of love. I didn't know how I would or could go on. My life was nothing but an ever spinning carousel of pain, loss, and heartache. I didn't know how to stop it or how to get off. All I knew was that I was cursed--born cursed--and would die cursed.

Chapter Fourteen

I had no idea how many days I was on the couch. All I knew was that I smelled horrible, and I didn't even care. I got up, dragging myself into the bedroom that Gordon and I had once shared. Walking into the closet, taking one of his shirts off the hanger, I slowly slipped it on. Wanting Gordon with me any way that I could have him, I opened up his laundry bin, picking up a handful of his clothes sniffing them. One of his jackets that I hadn't got the chance to take to the cleaners was on top of the island. When I picked it up, it smelled just like Gordon's favorite cologne. I took the sleeves, placing them around my neck, pretending like I was holding him close to me. I rested my head in the collar, letting my nose take all of the aroma that reminded me of him. I could still remember his touch, how he would whisper in my ear, kiss my neck, and make passionate love to me. I thought of how he would grab me and dance with me, with no music playing, just the sounds of love singing to him from his heart. He never ceased to surprise me, console me, and love me. My life was no longer worth living without Gordon. I knew I had come to my end.

I went into the kitchen cabinet, grabbing the bottle of Gordon's scotch. I walked into the bathroom, opening up the medicine cabinet, and took out all the bottles of pills, sitting them on the sink next to the open bottle of Scotch. I took a long look at myself in the mirror, I didn't recognize the reflection staring back at me. My skin looked dull. There was no life left in my eyes. The replenished me I had grown to love was gone. She, too, had died with Gordon. I took a large swig of the Scotch. It burned the back of my throat, warming my insides. I took another swig. Then, I coughed. I wiped my mouth with the back of my hand then slammed the bottle down on the marble sink. It cracked but didn't fully break. My hands were shaking as I opened each bottle of pills. I lined them up like dominoes. Not wanting to take them one at a time, I opened my mouth wide to pour the pills in. But something inside of me would not let me do it. Each time I tried, I failed.

'Why, why? Oh, God, why did this have to happened to me? Why did You take the only person that truly loved me? You knew that he loved me! What have I done to You for You to give me a life like this? If You hate me so bad, why did You even let me be born? Why do You keep putting me through this agony? You won't even let me free myself from myself, to end all this heartache and pain! Damn You! I hate You!' I slapped all the pill bottles on to the bathroom floor. I took my fist, reached back, and punched the glass mirror with all my might; it shattered. Blood dripped from my knuckles. The pain in my heart was far greater, and it wouldn't allow me to feel the pain in my hand. I took the already cracked bottle of Scotch, pushing it into the sink. I picked up the sharp broken bottle top, placing the pointy tip up to my neck.

Go ahead do it! Do it! I heard a soft voice inside of me say.

I stuck the tip of the bottle into my neck. My blood dripped down on to the deep crease of it. I closed my eyes, letting out a sigh, hoping to push it a little deeper, to drag it around my neck, wanting to puncture my jugular vein, desiring to bleed to death.

I opened my eyes, looking up to the ceiling. *"I can't! God, I can't!"* I raised my shaking hands above my head.

I fell on to the bathroom floor, wailing from the depths of my soul.

* * *

It was Saturday morning. Instead of getting ready to go to Australia with Gordon, I was going to his funeral. It took all the strength that I had to get up and get into the shower. The tears that flowed from my eyes had mixed in with the cascading water that beat down on my face, leaving no trace to be seen. My heart was broken, destroyed, and scattered into little pieces. It felt like I was having an out-of-body experience. Me, standing on the outside of myself, looking into desolate me, wanting to help myself but not knowing how. My body was so weak. I couldn't eat. I couldn't sleep. My heart was as dark as the black suit that hung on my body. My thoughts of Gordon shifted for a moment, when I heard a knock at the door. I dragged my body over to it.

"Miss, I am here to drive you to Mr. Gordon Lenox's funeral. Please take your time, I will be waiting in the limo." The limo driver touched the tip of his hat, walking away. Seeing the driver make that gesture brought back memories of when I first met Gordon, how he too, did that to me. It was something that I had never forgotten. The limo driver was the same man that came to let me know the day of Gordon's funeral. He also brought me an array of dresses and suits to choose from to wear on that day. The day that I dreaded was here. I never did ask him his name. All I knew was that he must have worked for Gordon. I wiped the tears from my eyes, let out a deep sigh and checked my eye makeup. I placed the pearl necklace that Gordon had given me around my neck. I placed my big wide-brimmed black hat on my head, slipped on my sunglasses, grabbed my purse, then slowly walked out the door.

When the driver and I pulled up to the funeral home, there was a man standing outside on the steps. The limo driver helped me out of the limo. The man walked towards me.

"Hello, Lena, my name is David. Gordon and I have been good friends for many years. I have heard so much about you." David reached out his hand.

David was a tall, extremely attractive dark-skinned man. His hair was cut short and wavy. It connected to his sideburns and his closely shaven beard. From the size of him, he looked like he could have been a professional linebacker. His shoulders were broad and his body was built. You could see the definition of his arms and chest underneath his dark blue jacket.

"Really? Gordon never mention anything to me about you before." I squinted my eyes.

"Gordon was a busy man. Maybe it slipped his mind."

"Not only a busy man, but a good man, the best man I ever had." My lips trembled.

"Well, I know that Gordon loved you. He talked about you all the time." David's voice slightly quivered.

I was unable to speak. My eyes filled with tears, I quickly grabbed a tissue from my oversized clutch to catch them before they rolled down my face, making a mess of my makeup.

David escorted me inside. I took a deep breath.

"Please don't leave my side. I'm a little afraid that I might pass out." I held on tightly to David's muscular arm. He held on to the top of my hand, assuring me that he was going to be right here with me.

David walked me up to the casket to see Gordon. When I looked at him, he didn't look the same. He didn't look like the man that I loved. The life that lit up his face was now gone. My grandmother told me that, when the soul leaves the body, they never look the same. Now, I know what she meant. Nothing was there but an outer shell of who Gordon was. My mind longed to believe that this was a nightmare. I longed for someone to slap me, punch me, anything to wake me up. There was no way this was happening to me. I so wanted to believe that, in a moment, I would be waking up with Gordon next to me. I would grab him, pulling my body close to his, never wanting to let him go. I would feel the softness of his moist lips touching my forehead, reassuring me of his love. I wanted to shake him, to wake him up, then see him turn to me giving me one of his sweet grins, like he always did. I wanted to hear him call my name, to tell me he loved me, to make love to me. I knelt down in front of Gordon's casket. I placed my shaking hand on the top of his cold hand. I broke down into tears. I wanted to crawl into the casket with him, to lay with him. I wanted to be wherever he was. My king was dead and gone, taking the biggest part of me with him, leaving me here alone. I didn't want to live without him. I couldn't feel my legs; my body was drained. David helped me up. Before walking away, I took the last bit of strength

I had to bend down to kiss Gordon's cold lips.

"Goodbye, my love." I whispered near Gordon's ear.

David took me to the back of the room, sat me down, handing me a glass of water. From the shaking of my hand, the water in the glass made tiny ripples.

While sitting, I noticed a well-dressed woman standing up by Gordon's casket. She was crying. She bent down, kissing Gordon's face, then she sat in the front row. David slid his hand down the front of his tie. He excused himself for a moment as he went up to her, he began talking, then pointed towards the back of the room where I was sitting. The woman turned around, lowered her shades, staring in my direction. She got up and walked down a hallway. David walked to the back of the room towards me.

"Lena, please come with me." David whispered.

"What is this about?" I asked curiously.

"Please Lena, everything will be explained to you." David held out his hand helping me stand up.

I didn't know why David asked me to go with him, all I knew was I was thankful that I had put my piece in my clutch. Gordon made sure that I had a gun in my possession, just like he did. He had taken me many times to the shooting gallery to teach me how to use it. He would tell me that a gun is power and the greatest form of protection. I stood up, slipping my opened clutch under my arm, gracefully as I could I followed David to a backroom.

"Please, have a seat." David assisted me into a high back leather chair then headed back to the door.

"What's going on?" I asked,

David never answered me.

I placed my Alexander McQueen printed satin clutch on my lap with the opening facing me. I put my gun right at the tip just in case I had to use it.

David came back in the room, this time he was not alone. The woman that kissed Gordon that was sitting in the front row was with him.

The woman sat down behind the large, black marble desk. She was cinnamon-brown in complexion, with a very pretty face, and striking features. You could tell that time had diminished some of her beauty. She wore a lot of makeup, like she was trying to hold on to her youthful appearance. Her salt-and-pepper hair was in a tight bun. For an older woman, she was in good shape. She was thin but thick in all the places that most women wanted to be. All the diamonds that she wore were a dead giveaway that she had plenty of money. I recognized that some of her jewelry came from Tiffany & Co. Gordon had given me a few of those same pieces that she had on.

"So, your Lena. Hmm, he always did like'em young and tender." The woman gave me a smirk, taking off her Gucci sunglasses, looking deeply at me then over at David who snickered.

"What do you mean by that? And who the hell are you?" I said curiously.

"And she's got a temper. She reminds me of myself in my younger days." The woman intertwined her fingers, exposing her long red fingernails.

"Let me get to the point. My name is Candice, Candice LaRouge Lenox." She leaned forward.

"Okay, so your Gordon's sister. What do you want with me?" I folded my arms.

"Sister!" Candice chuckled, leaning back, resting her head on the high-back chair. With a straight face, she eased her body back up. "Oh, no sweetheart, you are incorrect. See sweetie, I am his wife!" Candice raised one of her eyebrows.

"Wife? You're a damn liar! My Gordon was not married. As a matter of fact, we were planning on getting married when we came back from our vacation!" I held back my tears.

Candice let out a soft, yet fake, laugh. "Oh, how sweet! You are too cute for words! Lena, let me ask you this, have you ever been to Gordon's house before?" Candice asked slowly, while resting her on her chin on her half closed fist. She bent her body towards me, looking at me as if I was too stupid to comprehend her question.

"No."

"Don't you find that strange, that a man that is supposedly so into you and is about to make you his wife never took you to his house?" Candice smirked as she tapped her long red nails on the desk, waiting for my response.

"I didn't care about that."

"Obviously." Candice looked at her nails, then quickly up at me.

"I know that Gordon loved me with all his heart. And he would never hurt me in anyway."

"You are so young and so foolish, if you thought that my husband loved you. Gordon was a man that loved money, expensive cars, and pretty young women, like yourself. You were not the only woman he had. There were plenty of them just like you."

My heart sank. I got sick to my stomach, throwing up what looked like green liquid. I grabbed a tissue from my purse, wiping my mouth.

"Damn!" David jumped back.

"Get someone in here to clean this mess up!" Candice waved her hand towards David to get out of her sight.

"Listen, whatever my husband was doing for you will no longer be done. You are on your own. As they say, "all good things must come to an end," and, baby, you're at the end of the road. Now, get the hell out of my office!" Candice cut her eyes at me.

The coldness of Candice reminded me of my mother. I could see the hate all over her face. I stood there for a moment looking at her, seeing right though her. I knew her without her even knowing it. She made something rise inside of me, a fight to defend myself against her. I felt no intimidation, just courage.

"Gordon might have been your husband, I don't know, but what I do know is that he loved me enough to leave your old ass. If he had other women, it wasn't when he was with me. I gave him something that you nor any other woman could never give him, real love, the freedom to love."

"Get the hell outta here!" Candice picked up a vase off her desk throwing it in my direction, hitting the wall. I was walking towards the front door when I ran into David.

"If you were a friend to Gordon, then he sure as hell didn't need any enemies! You are a damn backstabber!" I slapped David as hard as I could in his face with the butt of my gun.

"That's from Gordon, you no good bastard!"

Everybody gasped in amazement as I walked out.

Chapter Fifteen

Not having anywhere to go, I stayed in the condo that Gordon and I once shared. As the days went on, the more I missed him. All I wanted to do was sleep so that he could come and spend time with me in my dreams. I longed for him to come walking through the door to be with me, but I had to come to the realization that this would never happen again. The more I tried to get myself out of this rut, the more I was sinking deeper into it. I was able to manage to pay the bills for the first two months, but after that all the credit cards and the bank accounts had been closed. I ended up having to pawn most of the jewelry that Gordon had given to me. It hurt my heart to sell it, but I had no choice; I needed the money to survive. I had no lights, little food, and no money. I had to figure out what I was going to do, but with no one to turn to, my hands were tied. I was back at square one, alone, and depressed.

I got up, hoping that the water company had not yet come to turn the water off. When the water came flowing out of the pipe, I quickly took a shower. When I finished, I wrapped my towel around me. Walking into my bedroom, I was greeted by a man who was sitting on my bed. Frighten, I nearly jumped out of my skin.

"Who the hell are you? And what the do you want?" I screamed, holding on tightly to my towel.

"Calm down young thang." The man stood with his hands held up.

Just then, Candice came around the corner into my bedroom.

"Nice little place you have here," Candice said, looking around. She walked around like she was taking a stroll in the park, enjoying the scenery.

"Not you again!" I rolled my eyes.

"Yes, it is me again," Candice answered back sarcastically. "You got one hour to get your things and get the hell out of here."

I stared at her like she was stupid and out of her mind. "Candice, this is my place. Now, you get the hell out!"

"That's where you are wrong boo-boo! This condo is in

my husband's name. Being that he is dead, it now belongs to me. You got 30 minutes to be gone."

"Lies, and you know it!"

Candice raised one of her eyebrows. "Shall I make it 15 minutes?"

By the look on Candice's face, I could tell she was serious. I hurried up, got dressed, and packed whatever I could. Rushing down to the elevator, I quickly went to my parking spot to put my clothes in the trunk of my car. With Candice and her head honcho in tow, I pressed the button on my car keys, popping open my trunk.

Candice moved her pointer finger from side to side. "Ah, ah, I don't think you will be taking that Benz, deary." Candice slowly pointed at me.

I quickly turned around. Candice and her boy were standing right behind me. "What? This right here is my car!" I threw my suitcase inside the trunk, slamming it I walked over to the driver side.

"Wrong again, I have the title to the car." Candice held up a piece of paper and smiled.

I stopped in my tracks. Candice had come in, pulling the rug right from under me, and she was enjoying every second of it. I didn't even have time to think about what

I was going to do next. I went from living in a beautiful condo on the Upper Eastside of Manhattan, driving a nice car, to homeless, helpless, and eight weeks pregnant.

* * *

With no other options, I ended up at a local shelter. It was the only place that I had to go, and it was not the safest place either. Lying on a thin, hard mattress, my mind was in a fog of confusion. I did not know how I would make it out of here. This place gave me the feeling of being trapped. I hated the smell, the look, and the feel of the environment. I had no intentions on trying to make friends with anybody in here. I never went out of my way to speak to anyone. They had a few outreach programs, but I was not interested in any of them. The only time I would stay in there was to sleep and get something to eat.

A few of the girls there seemed to be content with living in the shelter. They would be laughing and joking like life was good, but not me. I couldn't see myself ever being alright with living in a place like this. They would brag about moving out, waiting to get housing assistance to get apartments in the projects, to have their men come and live with them. They would talk about the things they couldn't wait to do with those men, then high-five each other, bending over, giggling with joy. Their conversations reminded me of my mother. They were just living in the moment with nothing but partying and having fun on their minds. They did not think about the needs of their children, only of themselves. When I looked at them, all I saw was selfishness. They made me sick to my stomach. Their children would wear the same sad faces that I had worn growing up. Looking at those kids was a refection of me. They would watch me like they could see that we had some kind of connections with each other. There would be no words between them and I, no smiles, just long blank stares.

Most days, I would sit in the park, watching the children playing. I would rub my stomach, wondering what my baby would look like. Being pregnant was hard. I was always sick, but there was no way I was going to have another abortion. This time, I had the choice to keep my baby, and I was going to do just that. I tried not to be depressed but it was not easy. I needed a way to climb up out of my situation, I just didn't know how. Many times, the thought of trickin' came into my mind, but my baby inside of me quickly changed my thoughts about that.

I took a walk over to the Social Service Office to see if they could help me. Everyone of the workers in there treated me like I was trash. I gave them evil stares. Even when I had a part in Gordon's wealth, I never treated anyone like they were beneath me. The people working in that office could only wish for the life that I had lived. I sat there for hours. With every passing moment, I could feel my blood boiling.

When they finally called my number, a gray-haired, white woman walked me into a small room. "What can I help you with today?" the lady asked, adjusting her cat-framed glasses, closing the door behind her.

"I'm homeless and need a place to stay. I have no money and I am pregnant," I said, unfolding my arms, placing my hands on my non-protruding belly.

"And where is the father of the child?" the lady asked, not looking at me.

"He's dead." my voice quivered.

"What was his cause of death?" With tight lips, she looked at me like I was lying.

"A car accident," I lied. For some reason I just hated saying that Gordon was shot to death.

"Do you have proof of that?"

"No not really, just his obituary."

"I'll take that." The lady wiggled her wrinkled fingers.

I handed her the folded piece of paper that contained Gordon's obituary.

The lady quickly looked over it dropping it down. "Where was the baby conceived?" She looked up at me resting her fingers that held her pen on her chin waiting for me to answer.

"What kind of question is that?"

She twisted up her lips. "Miss, would you please answer the question."

"I don't know--in a bed." I crossed my arms in disgust.

It happened in your got damn bed. Stupid old bat! I thought to myself, rolling my eyes, smirking at the thought of it.

"Well, as of right now, you don't qualify. Come back when the baby is born. At that time, you can receive assistance." The lady flung Gordon's obituary across the table.

"What? Wait a minute, that's it? Listen, lady I need some help!" I grabbed her arm.

Her eyes widen. "Security!" The lady pulled her arm from my grip.

167

"Lady, if you just wanted to know all the places that I have had sex, you should have asked! Maybe you wanted to know our sexual positions, too! You damn freak!"

A security guard came in, removing me from the building. I snatched myself from his touch. "Don't touch me! Don't you ever touch me!"

"Calm down, miss."

I got up in the security guard's face. "You don't know me like that to be putting your hands on me!"

Furious, I plopped down on a bench. Tears rolled down my face. I wanted to disappear. I didn't know how much more I would be able to take. Flashbacks of my life began to race through my mind. In my anger, I jumped up, kicking the bench so hard that it toppled over before I walked off.

On my way back to the shelter, I passed an all-you-can-eat buffet. The smell of the food made me so hungry that my anger subsided. I took a detour over to where I saw a large group of people going inside. I followed them in.

"How many in your party?" the waiter asked.

A big, older man began pointing, his short, fat finger counting the people that were with him, not realizing that he added me. They walked over to their table, while I headed straight for the buffet. I piled a plate with food, took a seat and ate. After gobbling down the food, I went to the bread table shoving some dinner rolls in my pocket and headed for the door. On my way out I ran into Jackie from high school. I put my head down hoping, that she didn't notice me. I continued, walking past her.

"Lena? Lena, is that you?" Jackie smiled.

"Damn!" I mumbled to myself. I turned my head to the side, praying that she would just walk away. She didn't. I slowly turned around. "Yeah, it's me." I gave her a half-fake grin.

"Are you by yourself?" Jackie looked around to see if someone was with me.

"Huh, no, I'm not with anybody."

"Alright, come have lunch with me."

Before I could say anything, Jackie grabbed my arm, pulling me back inside the glass double-doors.

The waiter was going to sit us near the people that I had gotten my first free meal from. Feeling bad about what I had done, I asked Jackie if we could sit on the other side of the buffet. She agreed. Jackie and I ate. She talked for over an hour. After Jackie and I stuffed our faces, we left. When we got outside, a few of the dinner rolls I had stolen fell out of my pocket. Jackie looked at the rolls resting on the ground then up at me.

"What's going on Lena?" Jackie asked with a concerned look on her face.

"It's nothing, Jackie. Thanks for the food. I got to go." I started walking away.

"No, not this time Lena! I let you pull that crap in high school, but not this time! You're going to tell what is going on right here, right now, and I want the truth!" Jackie followed behind me.

I quickly turned around.

"Why you need to know everything?" I looked up to the sky; my lips trembled. "Damn, I hate this." I whispered shaking my head. "Jackie, I,.. I…" my words got stuck in my throat, my tears started to fill my eyes.

Jackie put her arm around my waist. Without saying another word she walked me to her car.

She drove me to her apartment. Just like me, Jackie lived in one of the roughest neighborhoods in the South Bronx, but from the inside of her apartment, you would have never thought so. It was small, neat, and cozy. We sat on the couch. I told Jackie about my situation. That was the first time I had let anyone into the part of my life that I shared with Gordon.

"With all that you have been through, you need to rest your mind." Jackie patted my leg.

"Yeah, I know, but I have to figure out what I'm going to do. I will not give my baby up. My baby's the only person I have left in this world."

"That's not true Lena. You got me."

"Thanks, Jackie, I don't know what to say."

"Say that you will stay here for a while, just until you can find away to get on your feet."

"No, Jackie, I can't. I have no job and no money."

"I didn't ask you for anything. I will not take no for an answer."

Jackie got up, leaving me sitting on the couch. She came back, bringing some blankets with her. She opened her pullout couch for me to sleep on. "Let's go, time for you to lay down. Besides, the baby needs a good night's rest." Jackie pulled back the covers.

I eased my body up. Slowly, I walked over to Jackie, whose hands were resting on her full hips. It felt so good to lie on a bed in a safe place. Laying my head on the pillows made me think about how I treated Jackie in high school.

I sat up on my elbows. "Thank you, Jackie, for

everything. I'm sorry about the way I treated you. You know, back in high school. I had a lot of problems," I said, feeling ashamed.

"Just forget about that, I want you to rest." Jackie smiled, waving her hand.

As I laid my head down, my body felt relaxed. My eyes became heavy. No longer trying to keep them open, I gave in, allowing them to rest, to let my mind do the same, for the first time since Gordon died. Before I knew it, I was fast asleep.

Chapter Sixteen

When I woke up, there was a guy sitting on the other side of Jackie's living room staring at me.

"Hey, sleepy head. You have been sleeping for a day and-a-half." Jackie handed me a glass of water.

Damn! A day and a half? I squinted up my face.

"Oh, Lena, this is my boyfriend, Ben. Ben, this is Lena." Jackie rubbed her fingers through his sandy-blonde hair.

"Hey," I said under my breath, not looking at him.

Ben didn't say a word. When I looked at him, he had a smirk on his face. I didn't smile back at him.

"I cooked. You must be starved." Jackie put her hand on her hip.

I chewed up the last piece of ice that rested in the glass. "Yeah, I can eat something. Can I take a shower?" I handed Jackie the empty glass that once held the ice water.

"Of course you can, silly," Jackie grinned. She brought back a washcloth, a towel, and a toothbrush, handing them to me.

"Thanks."

I went to the bathroom to get myself together. Standing under the water in the shower reminded me of when Gordon and I were kissing under the Cherrapunji Waterfalls in India. I started to cry, hoping that the water was silencing my sobs. Pulling myself together, I got out of the shower, putting on my clean clothes. When I opened the bathroom door, a wave of stream greeted Ben who was standing in the doorway looking me up and down. The look on his face took me back to when I was a little girl. It made my skin crawl.

I braced myself in a protective stance. "You got a problem?" I didn't move, keeping my toughness intact.

"Naw, but I can be one, if you like." Ben looked me straight in my eyes. His eyes went down to my hands that were balled into fists. He slowly lifted his head, giving me a smirk, before walking away. I eased my eyes down then fully reopened them. I knew he would be trouble, and that was something that I did not need right now.

"Lena, come and eat before your food gets cold," Jackie

said. She stood by one of her red kitchen chairs, like those mothers on television did, waiting for her child to sit down for supper.

"Sit right here." Jackie patted the back of the chair.

My intention was to grab my stuff to leave, but the smell of the food guided me to the chair. Jackie had cooked chicken parmesan, spaghetti, salad, and breadsticks. For desert she made cannoli. Jackie had taken Ben's plate to him in the backroom. I was relieved that he was not eating dinner with us. I had eaten so much that I could hardly move. Slowly, I got up to help Jackie clean the kitchen.

"Oh no, you have a seat on the couch." Jackie pointed her soapy finger toward the sofa.

After Jackie finished cleaning the kitchen, she sat on the other side of the couch.

"Listen, Jackie, thanks for everything, but it's time for me to leave." I played with the strap of my book bag.

"Forget it man, you have nowhere to go. Plus, you are gonna have the baby before you know it. So where you gonna go? Back to that nasty shelter? You gonna chill right here for a while. I got you." Jackie picked up my book bag, placing it in the closet.

Even though, Ben didn't like me, I had dealt with his

kind before. I didn't want a confrontation with him, but he was nothing that I couldn't handle.

* * *

Things were going well. I had landed at job at a supermarket for a few hours a day. I would buy groceries to help take the load off of everything Jackie was doing for me. Ben didn't come by Jackie's house that often, which was cool with me. Most nights, Jackie and I would play cards, watch movies, or play video games. Sometimes we would go to the pizza shop to fulfill my craving for pizza topped with pineapples and pepperoni. Then, I would top it off with some mint chocolate chip ice cream. Jackie thought I was crazy for eating that, but I loved every bit of it.

* * *

I was a few days away from being in my eighth month. From the size of my stomach, it looked like I would have my baby any day now. Walking had become more difficult. My feet stayed swollen, and when I sat down, I needed someone to help me stand up. Not to mention my back hurt all the time. When I got to work, I was feeling more tired than usual. I worked for a few hours, but my back began to hurt, so I asked my boss if I could leave earlier than usual. She looked down at my huge belly, shook her head, and agreed. I paid for my few groceries, smiled, and said my goodnights to a few of my coworkers that were nearby. Stepping outside, I heard someone call my name. I turned around to see who it was. Slowly, the sound of a cane tapping on the concrete came closer, stopping in from of me. My face was expressionless.

"Hello, Lena, it's been a long time since I've seen you. How's Robin doin'?"

I stood there in shock that Mrs. Patty would acknowledge me like we were long lost buddies. I didn't answer her. I just stared at her and her mouth full of rotten teeth.

"Oh, I see you havin' a baby." Smiling, Mrs. Patty reached out her dirty, wrinkled, frail-looking hand towards my belly.

I quickly dropped my bag, slapping her hand away from me. "How dare you reach out to touch my stomach? You ain't nothing but a got damn baby killer!" My eyes pierced directly into hers.

"Umph," A lady walking past said, mumbling under

her breath.

Mrs. Patty looked around to see if anybody else had heard me. "Okay now, settle down." She slightly raised up her shaking hand.

"Settle down my ass! You no good murderer! Don't you never, ever, as long as you have breath in your body, speak to me again!"

A man passing by picked up my bag, handing it to me. I thanked him and waddled away.

"I was only doin' a job," Mrs. Patty said, her head slightly shaking.

I waddle back over to where Mrs. Patty was standing, I got up her face. "I pray to God that you burn in hell for all the babies that you killed up in that hellhole you call an apartment!" Angrily, I turned back around, feeling victorious that Mrs. Patty didn't get the chance to kill this baby inside of me.

* * *

By the time I got to Jackie's house, all I wanted to do was to get off my feet and lay down. Jackie saw that I had trouble getting comfortable, so she gave me her bed to sleep in. It was Jackie's late night to work at her job, so I lay down on the bed to take a nap before cooking dinner.

I have no idea how long I had been sleeping when I turned around, to see Ben sitting on the chaise.

"Damn! You scared me! What the hell are you doing here?" I gripped my chest.

"What am I doing here? I should be asking you that," Ben smirked.

"Well, Jackie is not here so leave!" I slowly sat up.

"You know, everything was going fine with Jackie and me until you showed up."

"Don't blame me for your short comings, Ben. Jackie invited me to stay here. Now, beat it!"

"Who's gonna make me?" Ben stood up.

I could'nt get up quick enough on my own. I just sat there, hoping that Ben would leave, but he didn't.

"Here, let me help you up." Without my permission, Ben grabbed my wrist, pulling me up.

I didn't like the vibes I was feeling. I had to get to my knife, just in case Ben tried anything. It was in my book bag, which was in the living room. I went in there to get it. Ben was following me. Just as I tried to bend down to pick up my book bag, Ben stepped

in front of me, picking it up. He unzipped it. When he

looked inside, he saw my knife.

Slowly, he pulled it out, twirling it from side to side. "Was this what you wanted? Now, I know you were not planning on stabbing me, were you?" Ben took the tip of the knife and began cleaning under his nail.

"No, I wasn't gonna stab you." I stayed calm.

"I think you're lying." Ben took the knife, sliding it down my cheek. He then move the knife down on to my blouse, popping two of my buttons off. He moved it down to my belly, letting the pointy tip poke my stomach; I held my breath. When Ben moved the knife, I slapped it out of his hand. It flew across the room, sliding under the radiator. When I grabbed the handle of my book bag to hit him with it, he threw me down on to my stomach. A sharp pain shot throughout my body; I couldn't move. Ben pulled my sweatpants and my panties down in one quick snatch. I could feel him entering inside of me, raping me. All I could do was tuck my hands under my belly to protect my baby. He repeatedly raped me each time was worst than the first. I was lying on the floor for what felt like hours.

Not wanting to believe this was happening, I tried with all my might to remove myself from where I was. I thought of a beautiful meadow. I was running and Gordon was chasing me. He caught up with me, holding me close to him. He picked me up, spinning me around; my face glowed with love. He bent down, kissing and caressing my protruding belly. I placed my hand on top of Gordon's head. When I looked at my hand, I was wearing a wedding band. So was Gordon. He stood up, holding on to both sides of my face, slowly kissing me.

"Oh, my God!" Jackie screamed, dropping her bags.

Ben jumped up from on top of me.

"See, I told she couldn't be trusted!" Ben pulled up his pants.

Jackie slapped Ben in the face. "Ben, get the hell outta here! I never want to see your face again!"

"It's not my fault that your friend is a whore!" Ben blurted out before slamming the door behind him.

"Lena, how could you? I thought that you were my friend." Jackie cried.

"What? Jackie you can't be serious! Your sorry ass boyfriend raped me! What you should be going is calling the cops on his ass!" I cried, crawling to the couch to pull myself up.

"Lena, I can't do that!" Jackie wiped away her tears.

"You can't? Why you don't wanna put your precious

boyfriend in jail where he belongs? You are just as sick as he is!" I slowly pulled myself up to my feet, snatching my underwear and pants up. "You know what, Jackie? If you thought that I would hurt you after all that you have done for me, then you're crazy! You can just go to hell with that sick ass boyfriend of yours!" I scuffed my feet across the floor, holding my belly, grabbing my book bag. Slowly, I walked out of Jackie's place, never looking back.

Chapter Seventeen

Dragging myself a few blocks from Jackie's house, I sat on a nearby stoop. I was tired. I'd had enough. I was sick of all the men that had taken from me, people who I trusted betraying me, and my mother and father who never gave anything to me. All of them had robbed me of *me*. All my life I had been someone's doormat. They would rub the dirt from their pitiful lives all on top of me, smothering me with their sorrow, covering me with their pain. I lifted up my shirt and began to rub my black and blue stomach, hoping that my baby was alright. Not even yet out of my womb, my child had endure so much already. Coming into a world where the odds were stacked up against my baby, made me feel angry. It made me so angry, in fact, that I knew I had to someway beat the odds. I didn't want my child to have the type of life I had. I wanted to give my baby so much more, I just didn't know how. *How can I take care of a baby without being able to take care of myself?* I didn't have all the answers. I was already into deep water; it was sink or swim. I chose to swim; to make it to the shore; to be a survivor. I needed the love from my baby. That was all the love I could depend on. As I sat there rubbing my belly, reassuring my child that he or she had my love, I hummed a song to my unborn baby. I could feel the movement of my child with every caress.

All of a sudden, I felt a gush of liquid coming out of me. I shouted. I was scared. I did not know what was happening or what to do. I felt a sharp pain in my back. My baby was moving around, kicking me with such force. Holding my stomach, I realized that my child was coming. With no one to help me, I waddled across the street to an alleyway. Beads of sweat began dripping off my face. I was in so much pain that I didn't know if I should lay down or stand up. Separating my legs, I held on to each side of the brick walls in the alleyway and screamed.

"Please help me!" I cried out as loud as I could. No one heard me; no one came. Each contraction caused my screams to sound abnormal, something I had never heard came from within me. Once they subsided, I would cry out again for someone, anyone, to hear me.

My legs got weak from the excruciating pain I was feeling. I laid down on what felt like an old piece of cardboard that was next to me. With each pain, I screamed. My body was shaking. "God please! Help me, please!" I screamed out once again hoping someone would hear me.

It felt like I had been lying in that alleyway for an eternity. I felt so much pressure that I wanted to push out my baby to stop the pain that I was feeling. I fought to get off my underwear and sweatpants. I opened my legs and I pushed. With every push, my body trembled. I was screaming for my life. I could see a tiny glimmer of light. Someone was coming into the alley. It was a homeless woman. She was carrying a large candle in some sort of glass.

"Girl, what's happenin' to you back here? Are you alright?" Her eyes widen. "Lawd chile, you havin' a baby!" the homeless woman said, looking down at me from behind the flickering flame. "Let me go get you some help." The homeless woman started walking away.

"Please, please don't leave me here! I'm scared!" I reached my shaking hand out to her.

"Honey, I'll be right back. Hold on till I get somebody."
She walked away disappearing into the dark of the night.

It felt like my insides were being torn apart. All I
could do was make hissing sounds mixed with screams.
I kept pushing, digging my nails into the dirt, rocks, and
glass. I could feel them cutting through my skin, making
my fingers bleed. I tried to keep my legs still, but the
torturing pain caused me to move them uncontrollably. I
was soaked in my own sweat. I tilted my head all the way
back, looking up at the dark sky, with tears steaming out of
my eyes I pushed with everything that I had inside of me,
letting out a scream that rocked me to my inner core. I felt
my baby slide out of me. The pain had stopped; relief had
finally come. I let out a few deep breaths before I reached
my hands down, in between my legs, in the pitch black
of the alleyway, for my child. I picked up my baby. There
was no sound; my baby was lifeless.

"Wake up. Please, wake up. Don't leave me. I need
you," I whimpered as held my baby tight, close to my
face. I could feel no breath. I hugged my baby, trembling.
I began sob.

One again, life had slipped away from me. The only
one that I had any hope of loving me was now dead. It was

too dark to see my baby's face. I caressed what felt like a head full of hair. Once I got out of this dark alleyway, I too would be dead, joining my child, my other children, and Gordon. I have already died back here. My next move would be to physically kill myself; *I have had enough.* I wanted out.

"Miss, you back here?" I saw a flashlight shining in my direction.

I didn't say a word. My baby was dead, so no need for whoever was calling out to me to rush to come to get us. The man took my baby from my arms. He began CPR.

"No need for that. My baby is dead," I whispered.

All of sudden, there was a loud cry that filled the darkness of the alleyway. Like a song, it echoed off the buildings, straight into my heart. It was the sound of my baby, alive! At that moment, the rigor mortis that took over my heart had turned into vibrations of joy. Life filled my body once again. I felt the warmth of life, my baby's life.

"Miss, it's a boy!" The paramedic said, smiling through the light from his flashlight.

A woman paramedic was with the man. They both helped me up on the stretcher, wheeling my son and I out of the alleyway.

"See, I told you I would come back. You will be alright honey. Just take care of the that bundle of joy." The homeless woman touched my hand.

"Thank you for helping me." I gave her a small grin. I looked down at my son. Come hell or high water, I was determined that my son and I were going to make it.

* * *

I had no idea when we had reached the hospital. When I woke up, I was in a room. I looked on both sides of the bed, but I did not see my baby. I panicked. In my mind, I thought that someone had come and taken my son from me. I was scared. I didn't know if this was a dream or reality. I quickly tried to get up out the bed, but the pain in my vaginal area slowed me down. A nurse walked into the room.

"Good afternoon," she smiled.

"Where is my baby?" I shouted, bent over in pain.

"Relax, your baby is doing just fine. He is down in the nursery with the other babies." The nurse comforted me and helped me back into bed.

I felt kinda bad for yelling at her. I had been through so much that my first reaction was to protect my son.

"Can I please see my baby?" I slowly pulled the covers up around my waist.

"Sure you can. I will bring him up to you." The nurse gave me a warm smile.

A few minutes later, the nurse came in, rolling a tiny see-through bassinet. She picked up my baby who was wrapped up snug in a blanket, handing him to me. When I saw his little face, it gave me a sweet feeling inside. He warmed my soul. He was light-skinned with a head full of curly red hair. He opened up his eyes, allowing me to see his big green eyes for the first time. I was so surprised. They looked just like Gordon's. He had the tiniest, perfectly shaped, pink lips I had ever seen. He had small little red freckles on his cheeks and nose. I opened up the blanket and kissed the top of his tiny hands. I took my time counting his little fingers and toes. The nurse assisted me in placing him on my breast giving, him what he had given to me, nourishment. My son was feeding the needs that I longed for all of my life. When I looked deeply into his face, he looked like his father. He was the most beautiful baby I had ever seen in my life, and he was mine. The nurse stood there, watching me hold my son. "What are you going to name him honey?" she asked.

I slowly looked up at the nurse, then back down at my baby. "Elijah." I pushed back one of his red curls from near his ear. "Yeah, Elijah Gordon Lenox. That's his name." I closed my eyes. Calmly, I kissed my baby's forehead.

"That's a really nice name, really nice." The nurse rested her hand on her face and smiled.

Chapter Eighteen

Elijah and I had been in the hospital for a few days, when someone from Child Protective Services asked me where we would be living. I didn't want to deal with them, so I gave them Jackie's address, just until I could figure out what I was going to do. I had no idea where Elijah and I would live. I just knew that no one was going to take my baby away from me without a fight. He was all that I had left in this world. In the evening, a lady stopped by my room to ask me a few questions. She let me know I was not able to leave the hospital with Elijah without proof that I was able to stay with Jackie. My heart dropped because we had nowhere to go. She informed me that, if I couldn't provide what was needed, Child Protective Services would keep Elijah until I could get on my feet. I nodded my head, understanding what she had told me. I didn't allow myself to have a confrontation with her. If I did, they would not let me see my baby, possibly removing him from the hospital all together. So I stayed cool, agreeing to the terms.

* * *

I stayed up most of the night, knowing that the nurse would bring Elijah to me around 6:00 in the morning for his feeding. The night before I was going to leave, I had planned everything out. I made sure that I packed a bag with supplies that the hospital had left in my room. I emptied out the bin under the crib of its diapers. I went into the kitchen, loaded up on snacks, sandwiches and juices. I made sure that I had extra pillows in my room to make a makeshift-me lying in the bed. In the morning, I peeked out of my room to see that nobody was sitting at the nurse's station. I was afraid to leave with Elijah, knowing that I might get caught and would be in big trouble with the authorities, but it was a chance I was willing to take. I placed Elijah in my backpack, grabbed the other bag, and headed to the elevator. My heart was pounding the whole ride down. Every floor that we stopped on, I held my breath, praying that Elijah wouldn't make a sound.

Almost down on to the main floor, Elijah made a slight whimper. I admittedly let out a few coughs to cover up his sounds. Once off the elevator, I could see the exit doors up ahead. I quickly walked towards them.

"Excuse me, miss?"

Afraid someone was talking to me, I kept walking. As I reached for the door handle, someone reached out, touching my shoulder. I slowly closed my eyes.

"Miss?"

I slowly turned around.

"Yeah?" I held on tightly to my bag, ready to swing if he tried to take Elijah from me.

"You dropped this." The man handed me a washcloth that I'd had in my hands.

I let out a sigh. "Thanks." I took the washcloth from him.

I quickly pushed the door open, and walked out of the hospital without anyone seeing Elijah and I.

* * *

With no place to call our own, we stayed behind an old factory building. I made a us a makeshift house out of cardboard boxes. For a few nights we made out okay, until

193

the rain came, destroying out makeshift home. Elijah and I ended up sleeping under an overpass. At night, I would lay Elijah in my book bag on top of the blankets I had stolen from the hospital. During the daytime, I would stay out of sight. Sometimes I would walk around at night, but most of the time we would lay low, not wanting anyone to spot us. When the food that I had ran out, I would go into corner stores or Bodega's, stealing something, whatever I could. That was the only thing that my mother had taught me to do well; nobody could steal better than me.

* * *

One morning a lady had come up under the overpass. She was a heavy-set, light-skinned woman, dressed in jeans, a tee-shirt, and some tennis shoes. I had no idea why she was here. My first thought was that she was from Child Protective Services, coming to take Elijah. Out of fear, I hurried and tried to get my things together then run away.

"Wait, please don't leave! I have'nt come here to harm you in anyway. I just want to talk to you, that's all."

I stopped in my tracks. "What do you want?" I held Elijah tight up against me.

"My name is Mrs. Parker. I run an organization for young mothers and teen girls."

My eyes shifted, afraid. "Who sent you here? Were you following me or something?" I cradled Elijah a little tighter.

"No one sent me. I come up under here every once in a while, or when I can, looking for any young teens that might need help."

"What you wanna help teens out for? You getting something out of this? I never heard of anybody doing anything like that before." I wiped my hand across my nose.

"Sometimes in life, everybody needs a little help. The only thing that I'm getting out of this is the joy and fulfillment of knowing that I have helped somebody," Mrs. Parker grinned.

"People only help when they want something in return. You must want something. Well, I don't have nothing to give you, so just leave us alone!"

"I don't want anything but to try to help you, that's all. Here, please take this. This is my card. We are always available twenty-four hours a day, seven days a week, to help. If you need us, please give us a call. You and your

baby don't have to be out here on these streets any longer."
Mrs. Parker handed me her card, and a ten dollar bill.

I reached out my dirty, shaking hand. "Thanks,"
I said in a somber tone. I looked at the ten dollars, not
understanding why she gave it to me. She didn't know me
from a can of paint but gave me something to help Elijah
and myself. I looked at her card. *"Mrs. Parker Place,"* I
whispered under my breath.

I watched as Mrs. Parker began to walk back down
from under the overpass. I knew that Elijah and I had
to get off the streets. We had been out here for over two
months. I had done all that I could for Elijah out here on
my own. Trying to make Elijah's diapers last, he ended up
with a bad case of diaper rash. I would pile on Vaseline
to keep him comfortable, but seeing him like that broke
my heart. Due to my lack of food, my breast milk wasn't
producing that much. Elijah would cry, wanting more milk.
I would get upset when I couldn't give him any. I didn't
want my baby to suffer any longer. Eventually, something
would happened to us out here, I knew these mean streets
would do nothing but chew us up, spitting us out, with no
one giving a damn about us. I had to try to give Elijah a
chance. Even though I was afraid that she might take my

baby to Child Protective Services, I had to trust somebody. Something inside of me believed her, and I was willing to let my guard down for the sake of my baby.

"I need you now! Mrs. Parker, please help me and my son! Please?" I placed Elijah on my chest, rocking him, with tears streaming down my face.

Mrs. Parker turned around, holding out her arms. "Right now, sweetheart." She walked back over to me, hugging me. Then, she guided Elijah and myself down to her van.

* * *

Mrs. Parker drove Elijah and myself to a place where young teen mothers lived. It was a big, white house with many windows. The house looked too nice to be in the ghetto, surrounded by the decrepit neighborhood. It didn't fit in; it didn't belong. There was a big light-green and pink sign in the gated front yard that said, "Mrs. Parker's Place," done in pink lettering. There were big beautiful yellow roses around it.

Living in the ghetto, all you saw was broken down houses, abandon buildings, run down cars, potholes in the streets, and hopeless people. It was strange to see roses in the ghetto.

I stood there for a minute looking at them, admiring their beauty in a dark and dismal place. Their beauty resonated, bringing life to a lifeless place.

When we walked inside, the girls that lived in the house were cooking breakfast. Babies were in cribs, crawling on the floor, and some were in highchairs. It looked like one big family, something that I was not used to. I hoped that I would be able to adjust. They had playpens, walkers, highchairs, and toys of every kind. Everything that a baby would need, Mrs. Parker's Place had it.

Mrs. Parker walked over and stood in the center of the oversized living room. "Ladies, ladies, ladies, I would like you to meet Lena and Elijah. Please make them feel at home. You all know how you felt when you first got here. So, make sure you show them some love." Mrs. Parker said softly clapping her hands together.

All the girls said hello. They gathered around to get a look at Elijah. They all thought he was so cute, greeting him with warm smiles.

Mrs. Parker showed me around the house. It had a lot of rooms. Every room I looked into was neat and clean. She took Elijah and I to the room where we would be staying. She stopped in front of a closed door. Mrs. Parker eased opened the door. I slowly followed her inside. The room was painted light-blue. On the side of the room that the cribs were on, there were different colored seahorses and sparkly starfish painted on the walls. It remained me of the sea; it was colorful and pretty. The room had two full-size beds and two cribs in it. Everything was neat, clean, and well put together. Mrs. Parker gave us some clean clothes, towels, and toiletries. I thanked her. The first thing I asked for was the bathroom. Mrs. Parker escorted us to one of them. I gave Elijah and myself a bath, washing away all the dirt and grime of the city streets from the both of us. Looking at the drain, I watched the dark circles of the city's filth disappear, hoping it would never return. I got us dressed then headed downstairs for breakfast. One of the girls smiled, guiding me to one of the many seats around the oversized table. She and her baby sat down next to Elijah and me. They all bowed their heads, saying grace. I looked around and then closed my eyes, too. The same girl who showed me where to sit asked me what I wanted from off the table to eat, making me a plate. I told her and thanked her. It had been over two months since I'd had a good meal. It was a good feeling to know that Elijah and I were off the streets, living in a safe place. I felt like I could take a moment to breathe, to let my body relax and rest. After breakfast, I took Elijah up to our room and breastfed him just a little more. Then we both fell off into a deep sleep.

Chapter Nineteen

One of the girls that lived at Mrs. Parker's Place was named Tracey. She was a pretty light-brown skinned girl with big brown eyes. Tracey had a muscular build; she used to play track and field in high school. In her senior year, she was awarded a full scholarship from three of the top colleges in the country, but refused to go when she became pregnant with her son, Jody. Elijah and I shared a room together with her and her son, Jody. Jody was light-skinned with a head full of sandy-brown hair that Tracey kept in an afro. She showed me where everything in the house was that I would need for Elijah and myself. Sometimes we would take the boys for walks around the park across the street or just sit on the steps and talk. Out of all the girls in the house, we became the closest. We had a lot of things in common; we were the same age, we had dreams and goals we wanted to achieve, and our boys were born two days apart.

Tracey came to Mrs. Parker's because the father of her baby used to beat her. When she was pregnant, he had a habit of kicking Tracey in her stomach when he got mad. He never wanted Jody. He tried to make Tracey lose the baby every chance he got. He threw Tracey down a flight of stairs a few times, putting her in the hospital more than once. She would never tell who did it to her. The thought of pressing charges against him was out of the question. Tracey loved her boyfriend, hoping that he would change and in turn, love her and Jody, but it never happened. She got sick of the beatings and moved back to the projects with her mother. After Jody was born, Tracy applied for assistance for Jody and herself. When she received it, her mother demanded that Tracey give her all of her cash and food stamps to take care of the other people who lived in her apartment. When Tracey refused, her mother came up with a lie, saying there was not enough room for everybody, so she kicked them out.

Not having anywhere to go, she ended up back with her boyfriend. Things were going well between them for a while, until one night her boyfriend got mad because Jody wouldn't stop crying. He beat Tracey up, throwing Jody down on to the hard floor. He gave Tracey two black eyes and busted her lip all because she couldn't get the baby to be quiet. Tracey grabbed Jody and ran outside in the freezing cold with only her nightgown. Jody had on just his pampers and a onesie tee-shirt. She was afraid that she and Jody would freeze to death. Just in the nick of time, Mrs. Parker saw her and Jody sitting on a bus stop bench. She brought them to her place.

"If it wasn't for Mrs. Parker, I don't know where Jody and I would be." Tracey wiped her tears.

"Me, too. I know that I would not have Elijah if it was'nt for her." I looked straight ahead. My eyes became misty at the thoughts of what could have happened if my son was taken away from me.

* * *

One afternoon, Tracey and I decided to take the boys to the mall to have a day of fun. We packed up our strollers, snacks for the boys and ourselves, and headed for the bus stop. We talked and laughed with the boys while we waited for the bus. Once we got on the bus, Tracey's attitude changed. A look of fear graced her face.

"Hey what's wrong Tracey?" I looked puzzled.

"He's on the bus," Tracey whispered, peeking through her hair.

"Who are you talking about?" I turned my head in the direction her eyes had shifted to.

"Don't look over there. It's Jody's father," Tracey whimpered. She grabbed my arm. Her hand was shaking. "I gotta get outta here." She quickly pressed the buzzer on the bus to get off at the next stop.

"No, Tracey, don't get off here!" I reached out trying to grab her.

Before I knew it, Tracey was off the bus. I hurried to get off, but her ex-boyfriend pushed me out of the way, almost knocking Elijah out of my arms. I had trouble getting Elijah's stroller off the bus. The bus driver closed the doors and drove off. "Please let me get off! I got to get off!" I pleaded.

The bus driver opened the doors. I got out as fast as I could. When I looked up the block, Tracey's ex-boyfriend was pulling her by the arm as she pushed Jody in his stroller. I quickly put Elijah in his stroller, hurrying up the block. When I got to the corner, I looked up the street. They were nowhere to be found. I stood on the corner, wondering were they could have went. Then I heard someone screaming. I quickly walked toward the direction of the sound. It led me to an open gated-driveway, when I walked into the driveway, I saw Tracey's ex-boyfriend cutting her up with a knife.

"Hey!" I said.

"Hey, what? You shoulda kept mindin' your business!" Tracey's ex-boyfriend turned around, pointing his knife in my direction.

He started coming towards me with the knife. He had a wild look on his face. My first thought was to protect my baby. I pushed Elijah's stroller to the side.

"Just let her go! We don't want no trouble!" I held up my hands.

"Too late for all of dat!" He swung the knife in my direction. I jumped out of the way to avoid being slashed.

"What the hell y'all doin' in my driveway?" A big African-American man stood behind me.

Tracey's ex-boyfriend walked closer to me. The big man pushed me aside. "I wouldn't do that if I was you! You keep comin' 'cause I got somethin' for your ass!" The big man showed his gun in his waist, resting his hand on top of it.

Tracey's ex-boyfriend stopped in his tracks.

"Stupid bitch, I gotcha good! That's what you get for havin' them put me on child support!" Tracey's ex-boyfriend said, before he quickly ran away.

I ran over to Tracey, her face and hands were covered in blood. She was shaking.

"Oh Tracey!" I tried to comfort her the best that I could. I looked up at the man with fear and begged, "Please call an ambulance!"

* * *

I called Mrs. Parker; she came to the hospital where we were. Tracey ended up in the intensive care unit at the hospital. The man that helped us came to see how Tracey was doing. His name was Rock. He walked over to me. "How is she?" Rock asked.

"Not so good." I said rubbing my arms.

"I have a daughter around her age, and if someone ever..." Rock let out a deep breath as he looked down at me.

I stared up at Rock whose face wore a look of sadness.

"I have to go. She was in bad shape and I just wanted to check on her, that's all." Rock touched my shoulder, patting it softly.

"Thank you for everything, Mr. Rock."

He made a frown then nodded his head before taking a step. I watched him slowly walk away. From Rock's expression, I knew that it hurt him to know someone could do that to Tracey. I was glad that he came into his driveway when he did, or things could have been even worse. I might have been up here going through what Tracey was going through. Just the thought of both of us being up here made me wonder what would have happened to our boys if we both had been injured. They needed us, we were their mothers and nobody would love them the way that we did.

* * *

I made sure that I went to see Tracey everyday. All the girls at Mrs. Parker's Place helped take care of Jody and Elijah. At night, the boys stayed with me. Jody would cry, like he could feel that something was wrong with Tracey. He missed his mother. I tried to make him feel safe and loved just like I did Elijah. I would hold him and sing to him, letting him know that his mother would soon be home. One night, Mrs. Parker came in our bedroom. She sat on Tracey's bed.

"You know Lena, Tracey is not doing too well. The doctors told me that she might lose some of her fingers on her right hand. They also said that she was cut very deep on her face and that she will always have that scar. I went to see her this evening; she is still in a coma." Mrs. Parker let out a deep sigh. "Lena, I want to thank you for being such a big help to Jody and Tracey. I will keep praying for her. Maybe you should, too," Mrs. Parker softly said.

"I don't pray to a God who treated me the way He did." I looked down.

"Lena, I don't know everything that has happened to you in your life, but don't blame God. He loves you, you know."

"If what He showed me in my life was considered love, then I would not like to see what He would do if He hated me. He never loved me."

"I'm not here to preach to you Lena, but if God didn't love you, He would have not let you and I come together. It was His doing, not mine. Well, I'll keep praying for Tracey and for you, too." Mrs. Parker stood up, she bent down giving me a hug, then she walked out of the room.

My eyes stayed stuck on the door for a few seconds after Mrs. Parker left. I wiped away the tears that filled my eyes. Slowly, I stood up and checked on the boys who were sleeping. I eased my body back down on the bed. I looked up to the ceiling. I wanted to pray to God, but what for? He never answered my prayers anyway. My prayers might even cause more harm to Tracey than good. The more I would pray to Him, the more He let my situations stay the same. Sometimes things even got worse. God would laugh at me, and then slap me down with more pains and disappointments. He didn't have time for me; I was a waste of His time. God enjoyed seeing me hurting, seeing me get abused, and mistreated. I was His plaything, created only for His amusement. I just hope that God would not have the same feelings for Tracey that He had for me. Maybe, just maybe, He would let her live, giving her a chance to raise Jody.

Chapter Twenty

In the morning, I gave the boys breakfast, their baths, and had the girls at Mrs. Parker's Place keep an eye on them while I went to see about Tracey. I quickly boarded the train. As I sat down, I noticed a young lady across from me. She couldn't have been much older than me. She was rocking a young child on her lap. I grinned at the child. My smirk disappeared when the child snatched off the young lady's sunglasses revealing an enormous black eye. She looked at me with a look of sadness in her eyes. With a straight face, she slowly eased her sunglasses back on. As the train rocked back and forth, looking at her made me think about Tracey. I wondered if it was her man that did that to her. I was curious to know, if it was, was she still with him? Coming out of the dark tunnel the train was slowing down at my stop, I reached inside my pouch.

Before exiting the subway train, I handed her a card from Mrs. Parker's Place. The doors slowly closed. I looked back to see the young lady looking at me, squeezing the card in her hand, pressing it up against her chest. The train slowly began to rolled away; my only hope was that she would reach out and get the help that she needed for herself and her child.

When I got to Tracey's hospital room, I walked up to her bedside. I was surprised to see that her eyes were opened. "Tracey you're awake!" I got so excited that I forgot that I was in the hospital. I quickly covered my mouth, not wanting to disturb anybody. Tracey didn't say a word, but what she was doing was, was blinking her eyes. The nurse came in the room.

"How long has she been awake?" I asked enthusiastically, staring at the nurse.

"For a few hours," the nurse smiled.

I pulled up a chair and sat down next to Tracey, telling her about Jody, Elijah, and all the new things that they were doing. When I laughed about something the boys did, Tracey would give me what looked like a small grin. "Tracey, I can't wait for you to get out of this place. I really miss you, the boys miss you and everybody else does too." I held her hand.

Tracey gently squeezed my fingers. At that moment I knew that she would be all right.

* * *

Tracey stayed in the hospital for almost three months. The doctors tried to save her fingers, but she ended up losing her middle and pointer fingers on her right hand. Tracey would hide her hand, not wanting anybody to ask her what had happened, but no one in the house did. All the girls knew what Tracey had endured, and they didn't want to make her relive it. Tracey felt embarrassed about what had happened to her. She would blame herself for allowing herself to fall in love with a monster. She wanted Jody's father to love her so badly that she put her life and Jody's life in danger. In the darkness of our bedroom, I would hear her sobs in the wee hours of the morning. I would pretend to be asleep, not wanting to interrupt her cleansing process. Sometimes tears would roll down my face listening to her. Tracey would be whispering about some of the things she went through in her life. She would repeatedly call the name, "Bobby." I didn't know who he was, but he must have been close to her. She would hold her pillow, rocking back and forth like a small child. I wanted to help Tracey, but I didn't know how. The only thing I could to do was to allow her to go through whatever she was going through.

Looking in the mirror was really hard for Tracey; her butter-pecan brown complexion was covered with a large slash mark from her ear to the side of her top lip. In the streets it was known as a "telephone cut." When she first saw her face, she screamed to the top of her lungs, falling to the floor. Mrs. Parker and I comforted Tracey the best we could. The sounds of her screams had bought tears to both of our eyes. She had become so depressed that it was difficult for her to take care of Jody. I made sure that I was there for anything that she needed. One evening while giving Tracey a bath, she seemed more depressed than ever. She placed her wet hands up to the front of her face crying, "Lena, I don't want to live looking like this."

"Tracey, you have to keep going. Jody needs you."

Tracey turned her head in my direction. "Look at my face! Look at my hand! I look like a monster! Oh God, why did he have to cut up my face and take away my fingers? All I ever wanted to do was to love him! Give him all of me! For us to be a family! How could he hate me so much? I especially don't understand how he could hate Jody so much! He his is son for goodness sake!"

I wished that I had an answer for her but I didn't. I didn't even know what to say. I sat there washing her back, speechless. Hoping that the warm circular motions from the water and the soft washcloth would somehow soothe her, even if just a little.

* * *

Mrs. Parker made arrangements for Tracey to see Kelly, a psychiatrist, a few times a week for her mental, emotional and physical issues. There would be times that Tracey wanted me to go with her. Of course, I agreed. When I first saw Kelly, I was surprised that she was a psychiatrist. She looked to be close in age with Tracey and myself. She was brown skinned with big, brown eyes. She wore her hair in a small natural afro. Her skin was flawless, with a healthy glow. Kelly dressed very conservatively, but with style. She carried herself in a professional manner, something that I hadn't seen in young women our age. I was impressed. Being that she was in her mid-twenties, she specialized in working with younger people, feeling that they could relate to her. When Kelly was talking to

Tracey, she had no idea she was talking to me, too. A few times I had to excuse myself from the sessions and go into the bathroom to cry and get myself together.

One of those times while I was in the bathroom, Kelly came in. She saw me crying. "Lena, are you all right?" Kelly asked.

"Yeah, I will be fine." I wiped the corners of my eyes with a tissue.

Kelly turned on the water taking a few squirts of liquid soap, washing her hands. "I noticed that some of the things that I talk about with Tracey seem to affect you. Have you been in a similar situation in your life?"

"What if I have? You can't do nothing for me. I feel that all you do is listen to people telling you their business. Then they leave, feeling the same way that they came to you, messed up."

"Well, I do listen to them. Sometimes that's what people need in order to set themselves free from the pain that they have endured."

"You mean to tell me that talking about your problems can make you feel better? And change your life?"

"Yes, Lena it actually can. I have seen a lot of young people change right before my eyes. It's like a light bulb goes off in their heads when they realize why they are feeling the way they do."

"I didn't know that."

"Well, if you ever need to talk, you know I'm just a phone call away."

I slowly glanced up. "Thanks."

Once we got back into Kelly's office, she handed me one of her business cards. Reluctantly I took it. "Use it whenever you are ready," Kelly whispered.

Tracey looked over at me, batting her sad eyes a few times, giving me a small grin.

Some of the things Tracey had been through, I had endured, too. I was just too ashamed to discuss my issues. I would never be able to tell it all. Besides, no one would believe that all those evil things could have happened to one person. I'm amazed that I am still standing through all the craziness that took place in my life. I'm even more amazed that I am still able to give love. Sometimes, when those flashbacks from my childhood enter my mind, I have to think about my love for my son. He has helped me in so many ways. As tiny as Elijah was, he saved my life. He has no idea what he has done for me. As long as I am alive, I will never let my son experience the type of dysfunction that I have lived through.

* * *

It took Tracy a whole year before she was able to go outside without covering her face. When she did go out she would cover her face with hoodies, always keeping her head down. She would still hide her hand in the sleeves of whatever she was wearing. When she did expose her face, Tracey would only venture out on to the porch, but it was a start. The thought of people staring at her face was too much for her to handle. She was getting better, but her nightmares were strong and very much alive. Every night, she would wake up screaming and sweating. It had gotten so bad that Tracey would not sleep at night, only during the day. Then one day, just like that, the nightmares stopped, Tracey finally had a little peace.

* * *

After feeding Elijah his lunch, I laid down on the couch, watching TV, while Elijah was playing with his trucks on the floor. There was a knock on the door. I heard one of the girls run down the stairs opening the door.

"Lena, someone is here to see you," the girl said.

"Who is it?" I asked, rolling my eyes, not wanting to get up.

"I don't know." The girl shrugged her shoulders.

I had no idea who it could be. No one knew I was staying at Mrs. Parker's Place. My first thought was that Child Protective Services was coming for Elijah and to put me in jail for taking him out of the hospital without permission. I quickly got up and picked up Elijah, taking him to one of the backrooms with the others girls, closing the door behind me. I walked slowly to the front door. My heart was beating faster with every step.

"Hello, Lena. I know you probably don't remember me, but I'm a friend of your mother. I just wanted to tell you that she is not doin' too well. What I meant to say is that she is very, very sick, and…"

I placed my foot on top of the other as I rested my hand on my hip. "Oh, yeah, I remember you. You're one of those people that was always up in the house getting high, just like the rest of them. Whatcha doing here? And how the hell you know I live here? Did she send you to look for me? I tell you what, since you wanna be all up in my business, you can do something for me." I got up in the woman's face. "You can give Robin a good bag of dope and help her OD!" I pointed my finger in my mother's so-called friend's face. "Listen, don't be coming around here telling me nothing about her! You understand me? Now get the hell off this porch for I kick your ass off!" I slammed the door.

When I turned around Tracey was standing there.

"What?" I shouted at Tracey, lifting up both my arms.

I walked around Tracey. I went into the back room and grabbed Elijah, then marched upstairs. A few minutes later Tracey walked in the room while I was in the middle of changing Elijah's diaper.

"You know you should go see about her." Tracey gently closed the door, resting her body up against it.

I was not in the mood for a confrontation with Tracey, so I stayed quiet. Tracey sat on the edge of her bed.

"Lena, laying up in that hospital made me think a lot about life. I know your mother did you wrong. So did mine." Tracey eased her body back, folding her legs Indian style. "Lena, forgiveness is not for your mother, it's for you. You need to be able to go on with your life. There are a lot of things we can choose in life, but one thing we can't choose is our parents, as messed up as they may be.

Please Lena; find it in your heart to go see her. This might be your last chance for closure."

Something about the way Tracey spoke to me, I knew that she meant every word she said. Her words had touched my heart; they made me think about what she had relayed to me, but the anger I had for my mother was still alive and well.

"Maybe Tracey, but I'm not making any promises to go see her. She did a lot of dirty and hateful things to me." I shook my head.

"I know exactly where you are coming from. I lived a crazy life with my mother, too. I never told anybody this..." Tracey let out a deep sigh. "My mother had a boyfriend. His name was Bobby. He treated me better than my own father ever did. I loved him and trusted him like a father. But eventually Bobby and I had more than the normal stepfather and stepdaughter relationship. He told me that he loved me more than he loved my mother, that I was special to him; I believed him. What did I know? I was only 13 years old at the time. One night, while everyone was sleeping, Bobby came into my room and slept with me, taking my virginity. For few years, Bobby and I slept together. I wanted to marry him. One day, I confronted my mother about Bobby and our relationship. She told me that I was lying. She beat me unmercifully. When Bobby came in from work, my mother confronted him, he lied about the whole thing. My heart was crushed. My mother believed him, beat me up some more, then moved me into my grandmother's house. She didn't speak to me for a few years. I was her kid; she took his side over mine. I didn't know that what I was doing was wrong. All I wanted was to feel loved. My head became more messed up behind that." Tracey held her head down, wiping her tears.

There was a knock on the door. "Can I come in?" said Mrs. Parker.

"Yes." Tracey and I said in unison.

"Is everything alright?" Mrs. Parker stared at both of us.

Tracey and I both nodded yes.

"Tracey, can you excuse us for a moment, please? I need to speak with Lena."

"Okay." Tracey stood up resting her hand on top of mine, giving me a small grin before walking out of the room closing the door behind her.

Mrs. Parker had a look of concern on her face. "Lena, I know that someone came here to talk to you about your mother today. You know you need to do the right thing and go check on her."

I threw my hands up in the air, slapping them down on my thighs. "What is this, jump on Lena day? Look, Mrs. Parker, nobody knows what I have been through with that lady. I would appreciate it if you would just leave this whole thing alone. This is my problem. You don't know much about me and what I have been through."

"I know that Child Protective Services was looking for you." Mrs. Parker folded her arms, raising up one of her eyebrows.

I quickly looked in Mrs. Parker's direction. "How did you…"

"I make it my business to know about all my young girls. You are no exception. I took care of that, so you don't have to worry about them anymore. All I am going to say is that you need to think about taking some time out to see about your mother. I would never tell you anything that would hurt you." Mrs. Parker gently held on to my chin.

I removed my head from Mrs. Parker's soft grip. "She ain't never been no mother to me! She don't need me for nothing!"

Mrs. Parker grabbed my chin one more time, turning my head back in her direction. "Then, you go and show her what a real mother looks like!" Mrs. Parker stared me straight in my eyes. She let my chin go. Mrs. Parker stood up. Without uttering another word she turned, leaving the room.

Chapter Twenty-One

I could see all of them, the men that I longed to love, and my babies that needed my love. Before I could grace each one of them with my first kiss, they left the comfort of my arms. I saw my children snatched away from me. I reached my hand towards them, screaming for them to come back to me, but they didn't. They were floating away like lily pads on top of a crystal clear sea. The more I looked at them, the further away they got, until I could see them no more. I ran up the mountain as fast as I could. I moved like I was flying; my feet were no longer touching the ground. I ended up sitting on top of a cliff, hoping to get a glimpse of my children floating by. Instead, I saw each of the men that had a piece of me marching up the side of the mountain. They walked past me, not even acknowledging who I was. I could see parts of myself inside of them, fighting to get out, to get back to me. I screamed at them to give me my freedom. They had me, never letting those pieces of me that longed to dwell with me free. I lost them; I lost me. Each man walked towards the top of the mountain. Gordon who stood in the distance was waiting for them. They reached inside of themselves; releasing the parts of me they had stolen, giving the pieces of me to Gordon. Gordon's arms held all the lost pieces of me. Then he turned around, he bend down. When he turned back around, he held all the lost pieces of me and all of my babies. Gordon and my children were all crying diamond tears. I could here the echoing sound of each of my babies saying, "Mama." It sounded like a symphony- -high pitched violins playing. It was so beautiful that it brought tears to my eyes. Gordon held on to my children and the pieces of me, then they all slowly turned, walking away into a prism of bright light.

"Gordon, please come back! Don't leave me! Bring me back to me! Bring my babies back to me!" I ran towards them.

The faster I ran, the further away they got. I couldn't reach them. With outstretched arms, all that was left was the whistling of the wind. I was standing there all alone.

I was awakened by my tears running down into my ear. I slowly sat up, wiping the tears that rolled down my face. I eased my body off the bed to check to see if Elijah was still in his crib. I looked down at the peacefulness on my son's face, kissing his soft cheek.

* * *

It took me three weeks to decide to go see about my mother. When I got to her house, I knocked on the door, but no one answered. I was about to leave, when I knocked one more time. The door opened slightly. I took a deep breath.

"Hello?" I peeked inside. I slid my body inside though the tiny opening of the door. Inside, my mother's house was beyond dirty--it was filthy. There were newspapers all over the coffee table and the floor. Plates that had dried-up food on them sat on the floor and on top of the television. The sounds of flies could be heard throughout the living room. The entertainment center was broken into pieces on the floor where it once stood. My mother's favorite spot, the couch, was now old, dingy, and tattered. When I got to my mother's bedroom, her bed was unmade, the sheets were stained. There were food containers scattered in different areas of her bed. Her ashtrays were overflowing with cigarette butts. The dust was so thick on her dresser that you could write your name in it. Her bedroom floor was covered with clothes, shoes, and anything else she decided not to pick up. I walked, kicking the mess out of my way, making a path towards the kitchen. When I reached the doorway of the kitchen, the smell of spoiled food slapped me in the face. Out of all the mess that she had on the kitchen table, my eyes zoomed in on my mother's "works" that she used to get high.

There was a woman standing at the kitchen sink. Her back was turned, so I couldn't see her face. It must have been one of my mother's "get high" buddies. She was frail looking. She couldn't have weighed more than 90 pounds soaking wet.

I tightened up my face, placing my hands on my hips. "Where's Robin at?" I asked the lady with an attitude in my tone.

When the lady turned her shaking body around, I could not believe that it was my mother. The little bit of hair she had on her head was undone. Her skin had the look of leather that had been lying in the hot sun. It was dry and cracked.

"Lena, is that you?" Her shaking hand lifted up to her dehydrated lips, taking a pull from her cigarette. The long ash on her cigarette fell on the floor.

I couldn't say a word; I just stared. The beauty that my mother once possessed was gone. What she was left with was an exterior that finally matched the interior perfectly.

My mother scuffed her feet across the floor towards me. Her legs got weak. She started to fall down. I reached out grabbing her. She smelled of urine. I wanted to let her fall down on the floor. I wanted to watch her crawl on her belly like the snake that she was. She was getting hers. A part of me was enjoying her looking the way that she did. For some reason, I didn't let her go, but helped her get into her bed.

"You want somethin' to eat?" she asked, holding my hand.

I snatched my hand from her touch. To me, it was as phony as she was. After all these years, now she wanted to touch me with some type of affection. How dare she! When I needed her love, she never gave it to me. She treated me like I was no better than a piece of gum that got stuck on the bottom of a shoe on a hot summer's day. I was the only child she had. She treated me like I was a curse, like my living caused the death of her being able to enjoy her life. When we got near her bed, I let go of her, letting her body fall down on the bed. She struggled to adjust herself they way she wanted to lie.

The real venom of death had come to pay my mother a visit. It had sat down; it was patiently waiting--and so was I. Death and I, looking joyfully into the eyes of my mother. I wanted to sit, to watch the show of her death, live and in living color. I wanted to see her suffer, to see her reach deep down inside for her very last breath, to see her not receive it. I wanted to watch her eyes bulge from the fear of death taking her away. I wanted her to hold outstretched arms for me to help her, just like I did as a child. To let her feel the rejection when I turn away, leaving her to die. I wanted to see the curtain fall down on the evil that would be no more.

My mother rubbed her exposed chest. "Yeah, they say I got that damn cancer. Of all the damn places I could get it I got it in my got damn coochie." My mother's laugh. Her laugh quickly turned into a cough.

I sat watching her cough; maybe this was it. Maybe she would die right in front of me. She continued to cough while I crossed my legs and watched.

"Lena. Water, water." My mother pointed towards the kitchen.

I sat watching her beg. My face began to reveal a smirk, and then I frowned. At that very moment, I had let myself become her. I didn't want to be in the image of her. I hated her. I had to show her I was more than she could ever be. I had to let her see the woman that I had truly become--without her. That through all of the hell she put me through, I came out of those ashes, victorious. I quickly got up, I ran into the kitchen to get my mother some water. Every drinking utensil in her kitchen was dirty. I shook my head, then rinsed out a glass. I held up her head. She drank what she could. My mother's arms were covered in needle tracks. When I looked at her face, she gave me a look that showed me her shame.

The remembrance of my grandmother arguing with my mother entered into my mind. *You better be careful how you treat that chile. One day you gonna need her to hand you a glass of water,* were the words that my grandmother had said. What she spoke way back then had now come to fruition.

My mother's eyelids had fallen. She let out a sigh, then slowly fell asleep. The lit cigarette that she had in her hand, I put it out in the pile of smelly ashes. I grabbed my jacket to leave. When I got to the door, I turned around. Something inside of me wouldn't let me leave her place in the condition that it was in. I didn't understand why I was feeling this way; I hated it. It made me feel like I was weak, giving into her needs, something that she never did for me. Never in a million years would I have ever thought to do something for my mother. For as long as can remember, my heart towards her had always been full of anger and resentment. I took off my jacket, placing it back down on the back of the chair, took a deep breath, and began to clean my mother's apartment, avoiding my bedroom. For it held way too many memories that I wasn't willing to relive.

Chapter Twenty-Two

"Happy third birthday, Elijah! Happy birthday to you!"

Elijah blew out his candles. Everyone at Mrs. Parker's Place clapped.

"What did you wish for, Elijah?" Mrs. Parker asked, holding on to his tiny arms.

"I can't tell you, Mrs. Parker, I might not get it." Elijah gave Mrs. Parker a serious face.

"That's right, baby," Mrs. Parker smiled, giving Elijah a kiss on his cheek.

After the kids had their cake and ice cream, we played a few games. The kids loved the clown that made them laugh while he created balloon hats and animals. Tracey and I started to clean up and put the food away.

The sound of small feet running entered into the

kitchen. "Mommy, can I open my presents now?" Elijah pulled on the hem of my skirt.

"Sure you can, baby." I bent down, sliding my pointer finger across bridge of Elijah's nose.

"Yea! I love you, Mommy." Elijah wrapped his little arms around my neck.

"I love you, too, baby."

Elijah's eyes got so big when he saw all the gifts he got. He ripped through the wrapping papers with excitement, wanting to see each present. He thanked everyone.

"Oh, Mommy, I got everything I wanted! Can I take some of my toys outside and play?" Elijah asked, jumping up and down.

"Yes, let's go." I gently rub Elijah's tummy.

Elijah, along with all the other kids, ran down the stairs, into the front yard to play. I lit a cigarette, sat on the porch, and watched. Out of all the gifts that Elijah had received, I couldn't give him what I wanted him to have--his father. He would never know the love that Gordon would have given him. My son was robbed of his father's love. The reflection of his identity had been stripped from him. Elijah had become a statistic at no fault of his own; he was born one. I could teach him the best that I could, but when it came to showing him how to be a man, I was helpless. It was something that I knew nothing about. The only thing that I had were photographs of Gordon that couldn't speak, That couldn't teach, that couldn't explain manhood to him--nothing. If his father were alive, he would be proud to call Elijah his son. I envisioned Gordon holding him, lifting his small body up in the air, smiling up at him, while Elijah smiled down at Gordon.

Looking at my son gave me a joy that was indescribable. His smile was as bright as the sunlight that hit his curly, naturally red, bouncing hair. I never wanted his smile to leave his face. I wanted him to be able to always be as free as he was at this very moment in time. I wanted to freeze it, put it in a jar, and give it to my son whenever he needed it. Elijah had become my world. I couldn't imagine my life without him. He was the sole survivor of my 14 children. He was the one who made it through the barriers, all the obstacles, and beat all the odds. I knew a day would come that Elijah would be out amongst the cold and cruelness of the world. He would no longer want my protection. The thought gave me a pinch in my heart. I savored every moment with my child. I didn't take a second for granted. I noticed the very fine details of his life. I observed each curl in his hair, each freckle on his face, the way his mouth moved, the blinking of his eyes, and the expressions that graced his face that reminded me of Gordon. Everything.

All that I do, I do it for Elijah. He would always receive love from me, all the love I carried inside of me. I would do whatever it took to make sure my son would had a good life, a life with some form of normality.. He would not be caught up in the destruction of hate, lack of love, or deception that I had lived through. I would be his warrior, battling for him until death.

I stood up when I saw a white car pull up in the driveway. A Caucasian man and an African-American man got out of the car. I watched their every move. The two of them walked up into the porch.

"Hello, I'm looking for a Lena Johnson," The African-American man said.

"What you want with her?" I squinted my eyes staring at the two of them.

Elijah ran up on the porch. "Mommy, can I have some water, please?" Elijah looked up at me.

Both men looked down at Elijah, looked at me, then at each other.

"Are you Lena?" The African-American man questioned.

"Yes, yes I am. Now, what is it that you want?" I held Elijah close to my leg.

"He looks just like Gordon." The African-American whispered. His eyes began to fill with tears, never taking his eyes off of Elijah.

"What do you know about Gordon?" I picked up Elijah.

"Lena, I'm Gordon's brother, Lonny. This is my attorney, Mark Letterman."

"Hello, Miss Johnson," the attorney said, reaching out his hand.

"Hello," I said, putting Elijah back down, shaking Mark Letterman's hand.

"I really don't know why I'm asking you this, but is this little boy Gordon's son?" Lonny asked curiously.

"Yes, it is. His name is Elijah Gordon Lenox." I looked down at my son with pride and smiled.

"Really? I like how you turned the names around," Lonny stated.

"What are you talking about?" I was confused.

"You didn't know? Gordon's middle name was Elijah."

At that moment, I knew it was not a coincidence that I gave Elijah his name.

Lonny slightly lifted up both of his pant legs before bending down eye level to Elijah. "Hey Elijah, I am your Uncle Lonny. It sure is nice to meet you," Lonny smiled at Elijah.

237

I looked closely at Lonny. I could see the resemblance between Gordon, Lonny and Elijah.

Elijah smiled. "Hi Uncle Lonny. Nice to meet you too." Elijah gave Lonny a hug, Lonny held Elijah, he wiped a tear that trickled down out of the corner of his eye.

Lonny stood up holding Elijah in his arm. "Lena, I came to discuss some business with you. Can we go somewhere in private to talk?" Lonny asked.

I smashed my resting cigarette down in the ashtray. "Yeah, sure."

We all went inside. I gave Elijah his water, sending him back outside to play. The three of us took a seat at the dining room table.

"Lena, I don't know if you knew this or not, but my brother left you a large sum of money."

My eyes widen. "Ah, no, I had no idea." Nervously, I played with my fingers under the table.

"I know that Candice did not let you know. I heard all about the run-ins you had with her, I want to apologize to you for that. My brother left me in charge of his estate, and I have been trying to find you for over two years now," Lonny expressed.

"Miss Johnson, here are some documents that I need you to sign so that we can release your money to you."

Attorney Letterman handed me a stack of papers out of his briefcase.

Everything was happening so fast that my head was spinning.

"Please feel free to read them over if you'd like. I will give you a few days to review them before contacting you," Attorney Letterman addressed.

"All right," I stated, still confused.

"Now, if you two will excuse me..." Attorney Letterman grabbed his hat, his briefcase, got up, and walked outside, leaving Lonny and I at the table.

Lonny watched Attorney Letterman walk outside before looking back in my direction, intertwining his hands on the table. "Lena, one evening Mrs. Parker was at my house for dinner. She and my wife are very good friends. She began talking about some of the girls in her home, and how fond she is of all of you. She mentioned your name. She talked about you, and I wondered if you were the Lena that I had been looking for. She told me that I was welcome to come over to see if you were her. This is truly a miracle that I found you." Lonny grinned.

In shock, I could not stand to my feet. Mrs. Parker came inside and spoke to Lonny and myself. "Lena, are you all right, sweetheart?" Mrs. Parker rested her hand on my shoulder, giving me a look of concern.

I couldn't speak.

"Lonny, is this the Lena you have been looking for?" Mrs. Parker's face lit up.

"Yes, Betty it is," Lonny smiled.

"The Lord sure does work in mysterious ways." Mrs. Parker raised her hands up.

"Yes, He does Betty. Yes, He does." Lonny hugged Mrs. Parker and the two of them chuckled.

I stood up after getting my bearings together; then walked Lonny outside.

"You know Lena, my brother loved you very much. He was in the process of divorcing Candice. They had been separated for many years. I wanted to clear the air about that situation."

I folded my arms. "Yeah, well she made me feel like Gordon had me and many other women. All I know is that the love Gordon had for me was real, nobody could fake that good."

"He gave that all up when he met you. Gordon wanted to be your husband. I know that if he were still alive, you two would have been married. If he could only see Elijah, my brother would be proud."

"Yeah, if only." I tightly wrapped my arms around myself.

Lonny placed his hands in the pant pockets of his suit. "By the way, my wife and I are having a dinner party in our New Jersey home next week. I would love for you and Elijah to come to meet the family."

"I will think about it."

Lonny snapped his fingers. "Oh, I almost forgot! This is for you." Lonny reached inside his suit jacket, pulling out a small, black velvet box handing it to me. I gave him a look of confusion, not understand why he had given it to me. When I opened it, inside was the biggest, most beautiful diamond ring I had ever seen.

"That ring was on Gordon the day he was…"

The two of us shared a silent moment.

"Lena, he bought it for you."

"Oh my, it's so beautiful. It must have been my engagement ring."

"Yes, it was. I had spoken to Gordon a few hours before. He told me that he had brought you a diamond ring. He was going to surprise you by popping the question when the two of you reached Australia."

I covered my mouth with my hand, my head slightly shaking from side to side. I tried not to cry, but the tears wouldn't stop flowing. Lonny reached out his arms, hugging me.

"Lonny, I miss him so much."I whimpered with my head resting on Lonny's chest.

"Me, too, Lena. He was my best friend." Lonny pulled a handkerchief from his suit pocket, handing it to me to wipe away my tears.

"Please take care of yourself, Lena. Elijah really needs you."

"I will do my best."

"Good, I hope to see you real soon. Hopefully at the dinner party."

"All right Lonny, thank you."

After Lonny left, I walked slowly upstairs. Holding the black velvet box in my hand. In the room alone, I sat on my bed. I stared at the ring. I wished that Gordon were here to place it on my finger. I wanted... desired... longed to be his wife. I would have made him so proud.

All of a sudden a ray of bright sunlight shined through the window. "I do," I said, looking up at it, it felt so warm on my face. I placed the ring on my left ring finger. I kissed it, then slowly I laid down on the bed, covered my face, and wept.

Chapter Twenty-Three

A few days later, Lonny picked me up to take me to see his lawyer, Mr. Letterman. My heartbeat became faster with every step down the long corridor. Lonny and myself stepped into to large office, sitting down. A few minutes later, Attorney Letterman came through the door, greeting us he sat across the huge table from us, placing his briefcase on top, opening it.

"Miss Johnson, I wish you and Elijah all the best." Attorney Letterman handed me an envelope then proceeded to shake my hand.

"Thank you," I said.

Closing up his briefcase, Attorney Letterman stood up. "Lonny."

Lonny stood up too, shaking Attorney Letterman's hand, grabbing his forearm. "Thanks, Mark."

As quickly as Attorney Mark Letterman came in the office, he was gone.

I held the envelope so tightly that my hand was shaking.

Lonny looked back at me, as he sat back down. "Lena, you can open it up. Take a look." Lonny smiled.

I slowly opened the envelope up. Inside, there was a check. My eyes kept shifting from one side to the other, reading my name and two million dollars, both written on the check. In shock, I dropped the check on the table, covering my face in disbelief.

"Now, you can take care of Elijah and yourself. I know Gordon is smiling." Lonny gave me a hug.

"I... I don't know what to say," I cried.

"Say that you will enjoy life, just the way you and Gordon wanted to."

Once again, my life had changed in an instant. I had no idea what I was going to do with all that money, but I knew I wanted to move to the only place that would always keep Gordon's memory alive in my life, Hawaii. We had fallen in love there; our hearts had become intertwined there. Gordon was the love of my life. I never wanted another man like I wanted him. He was my knight in shining armor. There would never be another man like him. Gordon had some huge shoes that most men were incapable of filling. He had left an imprint on my heart that made me realize that I would be with no other man. *Who could love me so deeply, with all my weakness?* I thought to myself. No one.

When I got back to Mrs. Parker's Place, I called Lonny. I spoke to him about my decision about moving. He thought that would be a wise decision. He informed me that he had friends that lived in Hawaii. He stated that he would contact them, letting them know my plans to move there. He would have them set me up with the best realtors, making sure I moved to a great location and making sure it would be a smooth transition getting us settled in. Later that evening, Lonny called me to confirm that everything was all ready being taken care of. I was impressed with how quickly he returned my call.

After hanging up with Lonny, I went into my closet. Placing a chair inside of it, I reached way in the back, pulling out the silver box that use to hold the cell phone that Gordon gave me. Even in its extremely tattered state, I loved that box. I especially loved everything that was inside of it. It was full of pictures of Gordon and me. Holding it gently, I sat on my bed, easing the lid off, looking at the photos. I smiled, laughed, even shed a few tears at all of the pictures of us. One of my favorite pictures of Gordon was of him dressed up in one of his many exquisite suits. This one was a black Newman suit. Along with it he was wearing an optical silk Versace tie. His chiseled chin was cupped in between his pointer and index fingers. In his other hand he held a Cohiba Behike BHK 54 Cuban cigar. He had on black and white cufflinks with his initials engraved in gold. His face was not looking directly into the camera. The light that shined into the room showed the splendor of his green eyes. Gordon looked so suave and debonair. I placed the picture up to my lips, closed my eyes, and kissed it. I moved the picture away from my lips once again staring it."I miss you, my love. Our son Elijah is now three years old. Oh, Gordon he's so smart, just like you. You would be so proud of him. I'm moving him to Hawaii, our favorite place. I miss you so much. God, oh how I wish that you were here moving with us." I placed the picture of Gordon on my chest, closing my eyes, I slowly rocked my body back and forth.

* * *

The day of the dinner party, Lonny came to pick up Elijah and me. We drove over the bridge into New Jersey.

I had been a few places but never to New Jersey and was excited to see how it looked, especially being that it was so close to New York. When we got there, we pulled up to a large gate. Lonny pressed a button on the inside of his console. When the gate opened, we had a little drive on what seemed like a tiny road that led us up to Lonny's house. The house looked more like a mansion. It was something that I had seen in magazines but never up close. We drove around the circular driveway that led us to the front door. Lonny parked, the three of us walked up the cobblestone walkway to the two large rustic-looking doors. When we got inside, there was a huge foyer with a large chandelier hanging down, in full view of the two sets of stairs that both led to the second floor. The floors looked like they were made of white marble. Lonny walked Elijah and myself down a long corridor into a sitting room.

"Miss, may I please take your jacket?" a maid asked. I had never seen a maid live and in living color before. I was a little stunned that African-American people had them. I eased off my jacket and removed Elijah's, handing them to the maid, thanking her.

"Lena, please have a seat." Lonny said.

While Elijah and I were sitting, a statuesque woman

walked in the room. She was the most beautiful woman I had ever seen. Her dark-chocolate skin was flawless. She wore a melon-colored dress that draped and flowed over her body like a second skin. Her hair was done in long, micro cornrows that she pulled to the side of her head, letting them flow down to her waist. Loony stood up, I followed, picking up Elijah.

"Lena, I'd like for you to meet my wife, Sasha."

"Hello," I said.

"Hello, Lena. It is my pleasure to make your acquaintance" Sasha's voice was soft with a sweet Caribbean accent.

"And this must be Elijah," Sasha smiled.

"Yes, it is," I too smiled.

"Hello, young man." Sasha reached out, touching Elijah's curly, red hair.

"Hi," waved Elijah.

Sasha looked, walked, and talked like the true essence of a black woman. She had a style and grace that I had never witnessed. Looking at her made me want to be a better woman.

"This is a beautiful home you have here," I said, looking around.

"Thank you, Lena. Let me show you around," Sasha said, holding out her hand for me to go ahead of her.

Lonny and Sasha had the most amazing home my two eyes have viewed up close. There was a huge indoor-outdoor swimming pool. They had a tennis court, basketball court, and even a movie theater. I knew that Tracey had never seen a place like this. I wanted to take pictures, but I thought that that would be tacky, not to mention rude, so I didn't. We went into a room that had a long table that could have seated 30 or more people. There was food lined up from one end to the other. All the dinnerware was gold with silver trimming.

The people started arriving. They were all dressed up; many of them had on diamonds and other types of jewels. You could smell money in the room from all the rich people that were there. The funny thing about it was that I too was rich, but I didn't feel any different. Maybe having money wasn't all it was cracked up to be. I was thankful that Gordon has left Elijah and I enough money to live comfortably, but I would never let it make me forget where I had come from. I wouldn't let my son live a life that made him feel that he was better than anybody else just because we had money. He would grow up with

249

a modest life. I knew that what we had today could be all taken away in the blink of an eye, leaving us penniless and homeless once again.

The people at the dinner party were very nice. They all introduce themselves to Elijah and I, making us feel very comfortable. We were all sitting down just about to eat dinner when Candice walked in. I lost my appetite. Putting my fork down, I let out a deep breath.

"Candice, what the hell are you doing here?" Lonny stood up, slamming his white linen napkin down on the table.

"Now, Lonny, is that any way to treat your sister in-law?" Candice took one of her leather gloves off.

"Ex-sister-in-law in my eyes!"

"Oh, no love for Candice huh? Now, how can that be when Sasha is my sister."

"Candice please leave, we don't want any trouble." Sasha stood up next to Lonny, resting her hand on Lonny's chest. He wrapped his arm around Sasha's waist.

"You're have a dinner party and don't invite me? Shame on you, sister. I'm not here to cause any trouble. I just want to join in the festivities, that's all." Candice gave a devilish grin. She looked around the room. When she saw me, her eyes got big.

"You!" Candice said, not taking her eyes off of me.

"Candice leave! Stop making a scene!" Sasha said, standing in front of Candice.

"You leave me out in the cold, yet you have the nerve to have Gordon's plaything here!" Candice flung her hand in my direction. "How dare you two do this to me! I am your sister! She's nothing to you!" Candice said. She walked around Sasha towards me.

My first thought was to pick up my fork and stab her with it. She was bringing up out of me my way of survival. I had to protect myself. If it meant doing some damage to Candice, then so be it. Then, I looked over at my son who was looking up at me, straight into my eyes, giving me one of his heart felt grins. At that moment, Elijah needed me more than anything. I couldn't allow myself to get into trouble. When Elijah showed me his beautiful smile, the thought of fighting Candice was instantly removed from my mind.

"It wasn't enough that you slept around with my husband, but you took all of my money, too! Everything that Gordon had belonged to me, not you! You got damn home-wrecker!"

"Candice, that's enough! Now, leave before I have you thrown out!" Lonny got in Candice's face, grabbing her arm.

"Get off of me!" Candice tried to pull her arm free from Lonny's grip.

"Lonny, she can stay, 'cause I'm ready to leave. Can you please drive me back to the city?" I picked up Elijah placing him on my hip.

Candice squinted her eyes then opened them wide, staring in Elijah's face. From the look on her face, Candice knew that Elijah looked just like Gordon. In shock, she froze.

"She had a baby with Gordon?" Candice looked at Lonny then Sasha. "My God, she did and you all knew about it, didn't you? Well, didn't you?" Candice screamed.

"Hi, I am Elijah Gordon Lenox," Elijah said to Candice, waving his tiny hand in her direction.

"Oh, my God!" Candice placed her hands in front of her mouth. She stood there, tears filled with black mascara rolling down her face, never taking her eyes off of Elijah. As the tears rolled down her face, she shifted her eyes on me, her eyes full of fresh tears. "You gave him something I never could," Candice whispered through her whimpering.

There was no need for me to express myself. My son's the face was conformation enough.

Candice stood there for a few more seconds. Without saying another word, she held her stomach. Slightly bent over, she slowly turned around dragging her hand across the dining hall wall, walking out.

Chapter Twenty-Four

Elijah and I would be leaving for Hawaii in a few weeks, I decided to take Elijah to meet my mother for his first and last time. I wasn't going to let her meet him, but I thought about what Mrs. Parker had told me about showing my mother what a good mother looked like. I wanted her to see that I did something that she never even tried to do. Elijah was my pride and joy, the one and only child she couldn't take away from me. A part of me was still very angry at my mother, yet another part of me wanted to rub my success with Elijah in her face. I decided to leave her some pictures of Elijah to see what she would be missing out on. I knocked, and then opened the door. We walked to her bedroom to see her laying in her bed half-asleep.

I held Elijah on my hip. "Hey," I said with very little

emotion.

She batted her eyes a few times before fully opening them. "Hey, Lena. Who's that?" My mother slowly lifted her head.

I looked over at Elijah, grinning at him, gently bouncing him up and down a few times. "This is Elijah, my son."

"Hey, Elijah. It's grandma," my mother smiled an almost toothless smile.

Elijah held me tightly, resting his head on my shoulder. "Hi," Elijah whispered.

"I heard through the grapevine that you had a baby. You can't always believe what these damn people say. If it was true, I was hopin' you might let me get a look at him. Whether it was true or not, when I found out, I got him a few things." My mother reached on the side of her bed, handing me a bag with some toys in it.

I was surprised that she thought to buy Elijah something. I had no idea she had it in her to think about someone beside her own self.

"And ain't none of them stolen either." My mother rolled her eyes then smirked.

Elijah dug down in the bag pulling out a baseball, basketball and a football.

"Elijah, what do you say?" I whispered near his ear.

Elijah placed two of his tiny fingers in his mouth, leaning his head to the side, giving a shy stare. "Thank you."

"Uh huh, you welcome."

My mother could no longer walk. She now had a nurse come in to take care of her.

"Lena, look in that drawer. I have somethin' in there that I want you to read. Just promise me that you'll not read it until you get to Hawaii." My mother pointed her shaking finger towards her dresser.

"How did you know I was moving to Hawaii?" I shot her a peculiar look.

"I have my ways of findin' things out."

Sitting in the drawer, there was a letter with my name on it. I held it up to the light to see if I could get a sneak peek. Before I closed the drawer, I saw the same card that I had gotten from Mrs. Parker when Elijah and I were living under the overpass. I knew that my mother had spoken to her. She must have told my mother that I was moving to Hawaii. I didn't say anything about it. I just sat back down.

"Promise me that you'll not read it until you leave."

My mother's voice was slow and shaky.

"All right," I said.

"Lena, Lena." My mother's eyes began to shift uncontrollably.

"Yeah?" I stared at her, not understanding what was going on with her.

My mother continued calling my name. She was looking up to the ceiling, not answering me. She had a strange look on her face.

"I'm so tired." My mother closed her eyes, easing off, falling asleep.

I stood up, looking at my mother sleeping. I pulled her covers up over her chest, I bent down to kiss her forehead. I quickly stood up straight, not understanding why I was about to kiss her. The fear of showing my mother some affection made me hurry up, grab Elijah, and leave.

* * *

When I got back to Mrs. Parker's Place, Mrs. Parker was outside watering her roses in the front yard. She was proud to have the only house in the hood with roses. Mrs. Parker said that you can bring beauty anywhere you go, even to the ghetto. She said that they reminded her of us girls, that we were once trampled roses. Now, we were blooming in the ghetto, each one of us becoming a woman, blossoming our seeds of beauty in the midst of our ashes. Most people in the neighborhood loved Mrs. Parker's roses. They would tell her how beautiful they were. They gave her great pride, but most of all, she loved to see people smile, even if the situations around them were dark.

"Lena, can I talk to you for minute?" Mrs. Parker put her watering pot down on the concrete stoop.

"Yeah, Mrs. Parker, what's up?"

"I heard about what happened the other night over at Lonny and Sasha's house. Please don't be upset with Lonny and Sasha." Mrs. Parker took off her gardening gloves, stroking the back of her hand on her forehead.

"They could have at least told me that they were related to Candice. I felt stupid around all those people. And you knew about it too, Mrs. Parker and never said anything. And what about you going to see my mother?"

"First, what was I suppose to say? I learned about your mother from the woman that came here asking you to go see her. She said that she had seen you come in here a few times and figured that you lived here. The woman told me that your mother was very ill. She asked me if I would go to see about your her, which I did. Your mother wanted to know if you were all right and I told her that you were fine. She said that she had heard that you had a baby, and I confirmed that you did. But I never gave her any information about Elijah, not even his name. It's my job to try to help out families if I can. I didn't go to her to hurt you, I just wanted to help, that's all." Mrs. Parker expressed before picking up her ice cold glass of water, taking a drink.

"That incident with Candice, I had no idea that she would show up there. Years ago, Candice tried to set up Lonny, saying that he wanted her. She almost destroyed Lonny and Sasha's marriage with her lies. When Sasha found out, she never trusted Candice after that. She was no longer invited nor welcomed into their home. Candice is a very vindictive and evil woman. She always has been. If I had any inkling that she would have shown up there, I would have advised you not to go."

After Mrs. Parker explained the situation to me, I realized that it wasn't Lonny or Sasha fault. I forgave them. Nor was I upset with Mrs Parker for trying to make things better between my mother and I.

I opened up the screen door. Elijah ran inside, and I followed, telling him to slow down. Tracey was laying down on the couch in the living room by herself sucking on a lollipop, looking dazed.

"What's up Tracey?" I asked sitting Elijah next to her.

"Nothing."

Elijah climbed on Tracey, trying to get her lollipop out of her mouth. He threw himself back, crying, when he realized he had been defeated. Tracey pulled out an extra lollipop, she opened it, handing it to Elijah, who got quiet as he started consuming the sweet confection. I knew Tracey well enough to know that something was wrong. I also knew that when she was ready she would talk to me. I backed off, grabbed Elijah, and went upstairs to our room.

Tracey came up a few minutes later. I quickly peeked my eyes in her direction, not saying a word. She laid on her bed, she put her pillow over her head and screamed. I placed my magazine down on my lap, folding my arms. I stared over at Tracey waiting for her to finish her temper tantrum.

Tracey placed the pillow down, looking over at me. "Lena, I know that you and Elijah will soon be leaving Mrs. Parker's Place. I just don't know what I'm going to do without you. You have been the only family that Jody and I have known. Ever since you came here, my life has not been the same. You and Elijah are all we got." Tears filled Tracey's eyes.

I scooted my body off of the wall, sitting on the edge of the bed. "Ahh, Tracey what you done gone and said that for?" My eyes became watery too.

Tracey was right. We were like sisters. She and Jody had become my family as well as Elijah's. She was there with me through some of the hardest times. When Elijah and I got to Mrs. Parker's Place, Tracey was the first one who greeted us with a warm smile, offering to show us around. There would be days that I didn't have the strength to take care of Elijah. Tracey would step right in, no questions asked. I didn't know how I could leave her and Jody. Besides, I didn't want Elijah and myself to be in Hawaii without someone to share the beauty of it with us. Elijah and I would have been lonesome without Tracey and Jody. The boys had become so close, like brothers from different mothers.

"Hell, Tracey wherever Elijah and I go, you know that you and Jody must come too."

Tracey quickly sat up. "Lena, you mean it!"

"Yeah, Tracey, I mean it."

We both smiled, jumped up hugging each other.

As soon as the check cleared, we would be moving out of the Bronx. It was just in time as Jody's father would soon be getting out of prison. Tracey was glad to know that she would be far away from him, not having to look over her shoulder in fear that he might try to finish her off the next time their paths crossed. We both wanted better opportunities for our boys. I wanted them to have the freedom to have clean air, crystal clear water, beaches, and blue skies. They would be able to go to school in wide-open classrooms, feeling the ocean breeze flowing through, learning to surf in the afternoons. We would all go scuba diving, stand under large waterfalls, and collect seashells. Coats and winter boots will be traded in for bathing suits, shorts, sundresses, and flip-flops. We would drink fresh coconut water and eat warm pineapple slices, letting the juice drip down our arms, soaking up our faces. Tracey and myself would take Hula lessons, pretending that we knew what we were doing, then laugh at how silly we would look. We would learn to water ski, go parasailing, and play golf with the big boys at the country club. We would open a small business selling trinkets to tourist, just for fun. We were on our way to paradise and nothing or no one was going to be able to stop us.

Chapter Twenty-Five

The night before Tracey, the boys, and I were about to move to Hawaii, Mrs. Parker gave us a going away party. Lonny, Sasha, and their three daughters came to celebrate with us. All the girls at Mrs. Parker's Place gave us cards and pictures of them and their kids. The older children gave Tracey and I handmade drawings. Mrs. Parker had cooked all of the favorite foods that Tracey and I loved. She even made her famous red velvet cheesecake. We all ate, laughed, danced, and even shed some tears. I was looking for Mrs. Parker. When I found her, she was in the kitchen fixing a plate.

"Hey, Mrs. Parker." I rubbed my hands on my thighs.

"Hey, sweetie, you enjoying yourself?" Mrs. Parker asked as she was scooping out a spoonful of potato salad. She stopped mid-scoop, smiling.

"Yeah, I am. How about you?"

"Yes, I am, but I'm sure going to miss you all. We have been together as a family for a few years now. I have seen you, Tracey, and the children grow up right before my eyes. Hmm, time sure does fly." Mrs. Parkers' smile faded.

"Yeah, we have been one big family. Time sure does go by quickly. We gonna miss you, too, Mrs. Parker, a whole lot."

"Lena, what's wrong? And don't tell me nothing. I have known you long enough to know that when you rub your hands on your thighs, you got something you want to tell me." Mrs. Parker giggled.

"Yeah, you do know me too well." I gave Mrs. Parker a tiny grin. I stood there watching Mrs. Parker for a few seconds, resting my head up against the wall. "Mrs. Parker, can I talk to you in my room?"

"Sure, Lena." Mrs. Parker put the plate down, licked the potato salad off her thumb, and followed me upstairs.

When we got to the room, I closed the door, having a seat next to Mrs. Parker on the bed.

"You know, I wanna thank you for everything you did for Elijah and me. I mean, if it wasn't for you, Mrs. Parker, I don't know where we would be today. You have been like a mother to me, the mother I never had. Shoot, I never had no father either, and you played that role in my life, too. You're a great lady, Mrs. Parker."

"Thank you Lena. It was one of the greatest things for me to do. I wasn't always right nor perfect, but I did my best." Mrs. Parker gave me a tiny grin, patting the top of my hand.

I quickly reached into my back pocket, slowly handing Mrs. Parker two envelopes. One of them had her name on it. "Mrs. Parker, these are for you."

"What's this?" Mrs. Parker asked, looking puzzled, she stared at me before she reached out for them.

"Please open them," I softly insisted.

"Which one should I open first?" Mrs. Parker looked back up at me.

"The one with your name on it, of course."

"All right," Mrs. Parker sniffled. When she looked at what was inside, her eyes got big. "Oh, Lena, I can't! I just can't!" Tears filled Mrs. Parker's eyes.

"You can and you will."

"Lena, this is ten thousand dollars!"

"I know what it is, and it's for you. You have another envelope to open," I grinned.

Mrs. Parker wiped a tear running down her cheek. "I can't take no more surprises today."Mrs Parker chuckled.

Mrs. Parker opened the other envelope. She slowly stood up in amazement.

"Oh, my sweet Jesus!" Mrs. Parker held her chest. She grabbed my hands, pulling me up hugging me. Oh, Lord, nobody has ever done anything like this for me in my entire life!" Mrs. Parker held me tight, gently rocking me from side to side.

"That's for you to be able to help a lot more girls like me. Mrs. Parker the world is full of girls that need someone like you in their lives." Tears trickled down my face.

Giving Mrs. Parker fifty thousand dollars to continue her work was nothing compare to what she had done for me. All of the things that she had done for Elijah and I were priceless. It was something that I would never be able to repay. She came to me under a dirty underpass, lifting my son and I out of the hell we had to live in. She gave me a smile that could light up through the darkest of situations. Mrs. Parker had given Elijah and I a love that came with no strings attached; it was genuine, straight from her heart. She had wisdom that she shared with me, never putting me down when I didn't understand something, never making me feel small, or less than human. In a loving manner, she corrected me when I was wrong, never backing down, even when I didn't want to hear it. She was not just a woman that helped young girls; she was an angel, a savior on earth.

In the room, Mrs. Parker opened up telling me why rescuing young girls was her passion, her calling. When she was just nine years old, her father was going to the store to get a pack of cigarettes and a quart of milk. He never returned. After Mrs. Parker's father walked out on them, her mother worked two jobs to support her, so she was never at home. Mrs. Parker's mother would leave her in the care of her family, thinking that she would be taken care of. It didn't happened that way. Mrs. Parker had been raped by several male family members. She said they would take turns raping her, tossing her around like she was a rag doll, without any thought about her feelings.

By the time she was thirteen, Mrs. Parker had been pregnant three times by the family members who raped her, never knowing who the father of her children were. She lost all three of her children due to miscarriages. She confronted other family members about what was happening to her. When she told them, they said she needed to stop lying, and they never wanted to hear her mention it again. When the members of her family that were raping her found out that she had told, they raped Mrs. Parker every chance they got. It went on for over eight years, until she ran away.

At the age of 17, Mrs. Parker met a man, Mr. Parker, who she had fell madly in love with. They had big plans on how the would spend their future lives together, longing to have many babies. By the age of 18, Mrs. Parker married Mr. Parker. He was a welder at a factory. He took good care of Mrs. Parker, buying her a home and even a brand new car. One evening when Mr. Parker was about to leave work to go home, a part of the building collapsed, killing Mr. Parker and several other employees instantly. Mrs. Parker was devastated; she had no idea how she would go on living without him. She would lay in her bed, spending hours praying to God for the strength to go on. It took time, but eventually He gave her the strength to keep going.

Mrs. Parker found a job. She worked in the day time cleaning a lady's house and went to adult high school at night. She graduated from high school then went on to college. While in college, she worked two jobs. She managed to keep up her 4.0 grade point average. Mrs.

Parker graduated at the top of her class and continued her education, finishing with a Master's Degree in Social Work, becoming a social worker. From that moment on, she has dedicated herself to the lives' of young girls. She'd been doing it for over 20 years and couldn't imagine herself doing anything else.

Mrs. Parker said it was her faith in God that kept her going. Even while enduring all the rapes, she would pray to God to help her. She knew that, without God, nothing in her life would have been possible. Many times she would talk to me about God. I never wanted to hear it, until she opened up, sharing her life story with me. I would have never have thought that Mrs. Parker's life was so hard, so full of pain. She was always smiling, full of joy, always had a kind word to say. She would tell us girls that the world didn't give her the joy that she had, and the world couldn't take it away. I just didn't understand how she could even give God any credit for the life that she was now living. He wasn't there when she was going through all those rapes. He didn't stop those people from hurting her. He let her husband be killed. How could He love her and let that happen? Mrs. Parker told me that God was right there all the time, that even though she went through

271

those terrible times in her life, she came out stronger. It led her to her destiny and purpose--to help young girls.

"What the devil meant for evil, God turned it around for good," Mrs. Parker said.

Those are the words that Mrs. Parker told me. They stayed with me. It made me think about my own life. I wondered if all the evil that I had experienced in my life, from a mother that never loved me, a father who never wanted me, all the rapes, the abortions and the miscarriages of my children, all of the men who I thought that I loved, to the longing for them to fill up the hole in my heart--could my life have a bright outcome? *Could some good come out of all of that darkness I went through? If that were at all possible, then how would it happen? And what would be the reason that I suffered so much?* It was something that I wanted to know. Maybe one day I would get the answer to all my many questions.

Chapter Twenty-Six

Tracey and I were so excited about moving to Hawaii we couldn't sleep. We both realized that it would be a whole new life for us and the boys. No more sounds of the trains over our heads; no more of the hustle and bustle of the city life. We would be leaving the urine-filled subway stations and the loud late night sounds for the tranquility of waterfalls, palm trees and ocean breezes. The first thing that I wanted to do was to slip on a bathing suit, sit by the crystal clear blue water, letting the wet sand get in between my toes. Tracey wanted a pina colada, to slip on her shades, and get a tan on the white sandy beach. Tracey had never been outside of the city. She was looking forward to new beginnings.

"Lena, I wonder what it's gonna be like." Tracey laid in a fetal position looking at me from across the room.

"You're going to love it there. It's nothing like you have ever seen in your life." I smiled at Tracey.

A part of me could not believe that this was really happening. All of my life, I would have never dreamed that I would have even visited, let alone live in, a beautiful place like Hawaii. Things like this never happened to girls like me. Someone who was born into a world of hate, violence, and abuse would more than likely become the product of their environment. People like me rarely find a man that loved them just the way that they were, through their flaws and all. Not me, a girl who has seen so many things that I should be in a crazy house, grabbing on the bars, looking into the outside world, not remembering what it was like, but yearning to know. Who would have ever thought that I, Lena Summer Johnson, would be a mother, a millionaire, a survivor. The odds were stacked up against me. I should have been a detriment to society, with no hope for the future. If my past could have designated my path that is the road I would have taken. Death would have been my first option. I had nothing to live for and no one to care for me. The miracle in all that I have been through lies in the eyes of my son, Elijah. He is my true definition of rebirth. Gordon, the man that I loved, had left me with the greatest part of him. The love of my life lives on. We live on together, weaved and intertwined into the life of our son, our most spectacular accomplishment. We did it together, in love.

* * *

It was 9:00 in the morning. Tracey, the boys, and myself were on our way to Teterboro Airport, in New Jersey. When we got there Mrs. Parker came over to me, hugging me.

"It's never goodbye, but farewell, see you soon," Mrs. Parker said.

"Thank you again Mrs. Parker for everything." I wrapped my arms around Mrs. Parker, holding her tight, as my tears rolled down my face.

"Mrs. Parker, I'm going to miss you. Thank you for taking care of Jody and me," Tracey cried, draping her arms around Mrs. Parker, she hugged Tracey back.

Mrs. Parker hugged and kissed the boys. It was hard for her to let them go.

"Always know that Mrs. Parker loves you two very much. Will you two draw and send me some pictures sometimes?" Tears rolled down Mrs. Parker's face.

"Yes, we will. We love you, too, Mrs. Parker," the boys both said.

"I love you all." Mrs. Parker blew us kisses.

We walked into the airport. For a moment I stopped. I looked back to see Mrs. Parker was sitting in her van, crying. In my heart, I felt that her tears were of sadness, that she would miss us, but they were also for joy and happiness for us. I eased my hand up at Mrs. Parker, she looked in my direction, slowly she did the same. I gave her a small grin before catching up to Tracey and the boys.

We had a nine hour flight. We were escorted to a much larger private plane than the jet that Lonny had booked for us. We were all excited. Tracey and I let the boys have window seats anywhere in the plane they wanted to get a good look at the view. Tracey and I sat on the sofa, had a few drinks, making a few toasts to celebrate our new lives. I had spoken to Lonny's friend, Marvin, letting him know that we should be arriving 4:00 pm Honolulu time. We had a brief conversation on Skype, exchanged photos via email and cell phone numbers so we would know who we would be looking for.

* * *

When we got there, Marvin and his wife Rebecca, were waiting for us. Marvin was a big, tall, handsome older man. He was dark-skinned with salt-and-pepper hair. His wife, Rebecca, was heavy-set with a pretty face. Everyone introduced themselves, before we headed to Marvin and Rebecca's house.

When we pulled up to Marvin and Rebecca's home, Tracey grabbed my hand in amazement. I tried to act like this was something I was use to, but I too was in total awe. I had never seen a house so big and beautiful in all of my life. It was bright-white, sitting on the plushest looking green grass I have ever laid my eyes on. Looking at Marvin and Rebecca, you wouldn't think that they were loaded. We pulled up into their garage that was the size of six large size apartments in New York City put together. There were all kinds of cars everywhere. Every one of them shined. Even the honey colored hardwood garage floors sparkled. The ceilings were high enough for a plane to come through. We headed inside the house that was even more spectacular. They had maids, butlers, even chefs. There was nothing for us to do but to sit and be served.

"So, did you all enjoy your flight?" Marvin asked.

"Yes, we did, thank you. We really enjoyed the plane, too," I said.

"Good. That was a Boeing 767 that brought you here to Hawaii," Marvin smiled.

"It was amazing," Tracey said, grinning.

"Excuse me, would you ladies like to lay the children down in their quarters?" One of the maids asked.

"Yes, thank you very much."

"Do you mind if we rest? It was quite a long flight," I asked.

"Please do. We will have Tessa come to your room later to see if you want to have supper," Rebecca voiced.

Tracey and I could have slept on the flight, but we were so excited, enjoying the amenities that the plane had to offer that we opted to stay awake.

Tracey, the boys, and I got up, following behind the maid to an elevator that took us to the second floor, to the rooms where the boys and we would be staying. Walking on the marble floors, we noticed that the house had many rooms. It was very similar to a hotel. The maid swung open the two large bedroom doors. The room had two enormous beds, sofas, televisions, and a large unlit fireplace. It was big enough to hold at least four of those cars that they had in the garage. We laid the boys in one bed then headed for the room across the hall where Tracy and I would be staying.

"Each of you has your own room," the maid said. She opened the doors to the two rooms next to each other. The rooms were double the size of the rooms that the boys were in. When the maid left, Tracey and I grabbed the boys. We ended up staying in the same room together, like we always did at Mrs. Parker's Place. This time we were all together, in one bed, and we fell fast asleep.

Chapter Twenty-Seven

I was awakened when I heard the maid, Tessa, speaking though the intercom. I reached over pressing the button.

"Good morning. What time is it?" I asked Tessa, while keeping my finger on the button next to the bed.

"Good afternoon, it's after 1:00, miss. When you are ready, please press the intercom to shower and have a meal."

"Okay, thank you." Letting the button go, I let my body fall back on the the extra plush pillows.

Tracey and I got the boys up, showered, and then dressed to go downstairs to get something to eat. I rang for Tessa. She came upstairs to get us, then took us downstairs into a huge dining room. Whatever we wanted to eat, the chefs made for us. While we were eating, Marvin came into the dining room.

"Hello, everybody," Marvin said cheerfully.

"Hello," Tracey and I both said. The boys waved.

"I have set up for you to see some houses today. We will see a few here in Honolulu/Oahu and then head over to Waialae Iki area." Marvin placed his newspaper on the table, then signaled for the maid.

"Ok, that would be great," I expressed, pleased.

The houses that we went to see were all so beautiful, but the one I fell in love with was in Waialae Iki. It was right off the beach. There was a huge guest house in the back that I would have considered a large sized home. Tracey adored the guest house, so I decided to let her and Jody have that house. Tracey was overjoyed. When I let Marvin know which house I was interested in, he called the realtor, assuring me that he would take care of it. I found it strange that Marvin never let me know how much the house cost.

* * *

A few days later, Tracey, the boys, and I moved into our new home. Marvin stopped by to see if everything was all right.

"Oh, you forgot to collect the money from me. I never

wrote you the check for the house," I said, reaching in my purse for my checkbook.

"The house has already been paid for. You don't own me anything." Marvin slid me the deed to the house.

"How could that be? And who paid for it?" I asked, placing my checkbook down on the white granite kitchen counter, confused.

"Gordon made sure everything that you needed would be taken care of."

"How would Gordon know that I would be moving to Hawaii?"

"I'm not sure Lena. Maybe the two of you had a discussion about moving here, and he remembered."

I dazed out for a moment, I looked out of the large kitchen window at the beautifully manicured backyard. "I don't remember us having a talk about that."

"Lena, a lot has been going on. It could have slipped your mind. Anyway, you have a brand new home on the beach that no one has lived in." Marvin grinned handing me his empty glass that a few moments ago held some orange juice.

Resting the glass in the sink, I was happy about our new home, but I still couldn't understand how Gordon knew that I would move here. I remember that, when we had came to Hawaii together, I told him that this was the most beautiful place he had taken me. Maybe he was watching over Elijah and me. He could have guided us here. All I know is that, ever since we got here, I could feel his presence with me.

* * *

Rebecca, Marvin's wife, took Tracey and I to all the upscale furniture stores. She also had a few of her own interior decorators come to our houses to give us some ideas. When we finished making arrangements for the décor for our houses, Tracey and I sat on the patio, eating some fresh fruit, while the boys played with their toys.

I pushed a strawberry around with my fork. "Tracey do you realized that no one asked me for any money to pay for this house or to furnish it, nothing."

"What? I wonder what that's all about. Did you ask Marvin?"

"I did speak to him about the house, but he told me that Gordon had taken care of

everything."

"Did you talk to Gordon about wanting to move here?"

Tracey picked up a piece of cantaloupe.

I squinted my eyes. "That's the strange part. I never told him that I wanted to live here. I'm sure I didn't."

"That's strange. I wouldn't worry too much about it. Besides, you have the house of your dreams, living in a place that you love."

I realized that Tracey was right, but I just didn't know what was going on. Something was not sitting right with me, with this whole situation. I decided to take a walk to clear my mind. Tracey sat with the boys while I went to the beach. I sat by the water, listening to the sound of the waves crashing. I closed my eyes, hoping to get a clear glimpse of Gordon. If Gordon were here, I wouldn't be feeling the way that I was. He made sure that everything went smoothly in our lives. I didn't have to worry about anything. The only thing Gordon ever asked of me was to run a few errands for him, which I was more than pleased to do. I didn't like feeling in the dark about what was going on. There were pieces to this money puzzle that were missing. I had no one around me who knew how to solve it. Everyone seemed to be happy for my new found wealth, but me. If I could have Gordon back, I would give up every bit of the money, down to the very last penny, to be with him. I missed him so much and wanted Gordon here with me. I missed how he would teach me things, how he would broaden my thoughts with his intellect, the sweet taste of his lips, the way he would rub my back, how he would make me know that I was his everything. Sitting here on the beach reminded me of how we made love to each other on the beach in Maui. Gordon had a way of bringing out the woman inside of me that I never knew I possessed. I was his queen, and he was my king. I wished that he would be able to let me understand what was going on. He had left me all this money, but people around me seemed to be walking on eggshells, not telling me anything. They were making me think that everything was in my mind, that I was imagining things.

* * *

When I got back to the house, Tracey and the boys were watching a movie.

"Tracey, we need to go and get us a car."

"When did you want to go?" Tracey looked back at me, holding a handful of popcorn.

"When the boys are finished watching their movie."

"Okay."

Before going to the car dealership, I stopped by the bank to take out a few dollars. When the teller handed me my cash along with the stub with my balance, I knew something was wrong. "Excuse me miss, but there must be some mistake."

The teller stopped working on the computer. "Yes, ma'am, what seems to be the problem?"

"You gave me the wrong account balance." I handed her the balance receipt.

"Let me take a look," the teller smiled, taking back the stub.

She slid the stub back to me. "No, ma'am, there has been no mistake."

"There must be. This account has over twenty-five million dollars in it."

"Yes, that's correct ma'am."

"I don't understand. I have an account with under two million dollars in it."

"I don't know ma'am, but this is the correct balance in your account. Would you like to speak to the branch manager?"

"Yes, I would. Thank you."

The teller escorted me over to the bank manager.

"Hello, I'm Karen. Please have a seat. How may I assist you today?"

"Hello Karen. My name is Lena Johnson. There seems to be a mistake with my account."

"All right Miss. Johnson, let's take a look."

I slid my account receipt across Karen's desk to her.

"Thank you." Karen picked it up.

"You're welcome." I slightly grinned, resting my purse on my lap.

Karen slipped on her glasses. She quickly typed on her keyboard. She stopped, lightly rubbing her pointer finger above her top lip while staring at her oversize computer screen. "Well, Miss. Johnson, the amount on your receipt indeed matches the amount that is in your account." Karen handed me back my receipt.

"How could that be? I transferred a little under two million dollars in this account."

"Yes, I see that you did, but the twenty-five million was deposited a few days ago."

"I just don't understand." I cupped my hand on my chin.

"Maybe it was a check you weren't expecting."

Is she for real? Who in their right mind forgets about

a twenty-five million dollar check? I sat there for a few seconds; my mind was racing.

"Is there anything else that I can help you with, Miss. Johnson?"

"Ah, no, no." I slowly stood up, placing my purse straps on my shoulder before walking away.

"Have a good day," Karen said.

I stopped and turned around. "What?"

"Have a good day, Miss. Johnson."

"Oh, you, too." I turned back around and continued to walk out of the bank in a daze.

Tracey and the boys were sitting on a bench. Tracey saw the distant expression on my face. She slowly stood up. "Lena, what's wrong?"

Stepping down in front of her, I slightly shook my head. "I don't know Tracey. I just don't know."

Chapter Twenty-Eight

My mind was so confused that I couldn't even think about buying a car. Tracey, the boys, and I went back home. I asked Tracey if Elijah could stay over at her place for a little while. She agreed. The only person that I could think of to call about this was Lonny. I quickly dialed his number.

"Hello?" I said in a somber tone.

"Hello? Hey, Lena, how are you guys making out in Hawaii?"

"We're doing fine. Thank you for paying for our flight here."

"I didn't pay for it. Gordon made sure of that."

I took the receiver from my ear, looking at it like it was some type of foreign object.

"It's funny that you mentioned Gordon. That's what

I'm calling you about. Lonny, Gordon had no idea that I wanted to move to Hawaii. When I get here, my house was already paid for and so was everything else. I went to the bank today. They informed me that a few days ago, someone deposited twenty-five million dollars in my account."

"You sound upset about that," Lonny chuckled.

"I just want to know where that money came from, and where did Gordon get so much money from?"

"Lena, Gordon was a very successful business man who knew how to handle his money. He made great investments."

"But how did that money get into my account?"

"Maybe Gordon set it up for you before his passing."

"That's impossible. He never knew I wanted to live here. This is all becoming creepy to me."

"I'll look into it Lena, then get back to you. Don't worry about anything, just enjoy life, and spend some of that money."

Lonny hung up, but his words did not sit well with me. My first thought was he was covering up something that he didn't want me to know. My mind was confused. Maybe I was just being silly. Gordon did provide a good life for

Elijah and me, and I wasn't even enjoying it. I've had so many disappointments in my life that I was waiting for the next bomb to drop, putting Elijah and I back on the mean streets of the South Bronx, where I had started. The only fortune I ever had was misfortune. That's all I expected to follow me.

* * *

That night I was lying in my bed. I didn't want to sleep alone, so I put Elijah in the bed to sleep next to me. Sitting up in the bed, I was looking in my backpack for the pictures of all the girls and their kids that lived at Mrs. Parkers' Place, when the letter that my mother had given me fell out on to my bed. I placed my backpack down on the floor. Slowly, I picked up the envelope, opening it, I unfolded the yellow colored legal sheet of paper.

Dear Lena,

If you are readin' this letter, chances are that I'm already dead. I know that I was not a good mother to you. Hell, I don't think you could have gotten one much worse than I was. When you were first born, I had high hopes for you. It wasn't your fault that my love for you turned to hate. I hated everyone, includin' my own self. Your father did a lot of mean things to me and to you. When I looked at you, I saw him. I wanted to kill the him inside of you. There were times I couldn't stand the sight of you. I tried to drag myself up out of that pit of hate, but all I did was pull you in. You be a good mother to Elijah. Don't cut'em him down like I did to you. I ain't ever had no love for God. I just knew He hated me. But when your life is danglin' on the edge of death, it can sometimes open your eyes. I have sewn some bad seeds. I know that this is a part of my harvest. I know that God has forgiven me. Now, my only hope is that you can find it somewhere in your heart to do the same, if not for me, then for yourself. I have never given you a real gift, but I'm goin' to give you a gift that no amount of money can buy. It's for you to ask Jesus into your life and into your heart, He is the only one who will be able to take all the pain away, just ask Him. Well, take care of yourself and Elijah.

Mom

I looked at the letter, balled it up, throwing it in the corner. My hands were shaking. I slowly got up and walked outside on to the patio, I lit a cigarette. I took a long drag, blowing the smoke out, I let the filter rest up against my lips. *How dare she tell me to just up and forgive her? She took everything away from me. She never gave me anything, not even her. What my father did to her, she took out on me because I was a reflection of him. I had to bear the brunt of her anger and disappointments, until it manifested into my own life. She just wanted me to wipe the slate clean, like a sandcastle being washed out to shore, like it never existed, just like that. Death was her cause to even approach me with a letter of sympathy. If her life would have been spared from the claws of cancer, she would have never tried to make amends with me. She would have been the same old evil woman she had always been, hating me because I resemble the man she opened up herself up to. Letting him penetrate the walls of her inner self, allowing him to ejaculate his lies and deception, mixed with me inside of her. I was floating, inhaling and exhaling amniotic fluid that was plagued with hate, animosity, and pain. She hated what they had created, hated me being inside of her. She pushed me out, hating me, into her world full of hate. How could God forgive her? He had seen all the things she had done to me, all the things her boyfriends did to me. And God only knows what my father did to me. What was I suppose to do, just brush all of that under the rug, like it never happened? Did He turn a blind eye to her madness? How could a God let that monster of a woman even be my mother?* I took my last drag, smashing the filter in the ashtray, sucking my teeth at the thoughts in my head. I went back inside, sliding the patio door halfway closed, allowing the warm breeze to fill the room. I eased back under the covers and laid next to my son. When I looked at Elijah, a tiny whisper came from inside of me saying, "*Look at what I gave you. I do love you.*" Not wanting to believe what I had heard, I snuggled close to my son and tried to fall sleep.

Chapter-Twenty Nine

I had given Lonny a few days to call me back, but he didn't. When I tried to reach him, his phone went directly to voicemail. I had spoken to Sasha, but she, too, acted like she had no idea what I was taking about. I decided to contact the realtor who sold me my house. I quickly dialed his number.

"Hello, may I speak with Mister Dobson?"

"This is he. How may I help you?"

"Hello, Mister Dobson. This is Lena Johnson."

"Hello, Miss. Johnson, is everything all right with the house?"

"Yes, everything is fine with it. I'm contacting you to find out how much was the cost of the house that you sold me?"

"I...I'm sorry, Miss Johnson, that information is

confidential. I am not at liberty to discuss that." The tone of Mr. Dobson's voice shifted to a lower tone.

"Excuse me? You sold me a house, but you are unable to tell me how much it cost?"

"Yes, that is correct."

"Shall I contact your supervisor?"

Mr. Dobson cleared his throat. His voice trembled. "Listen, Miss Johnson, I don't want any problems. What I can let you know is that it was just a little over a million dollars. Please don't let anyone know that I gave you this information. My job is depending on it."

Mr. Dobson hung up without saying another word. I knew that something was going on, but what.

* * *

I called for a cab to take me to Marvin's house to see if I could get some answers from Rebecca. When I got there, Tessa had me wait in the parlor. Rebecca looked surprised to see me.

Rebecca strolled over to me. "Hello, Lena, what can I do for you?"

"Hi, Rebecca. I'm here to ask you, do you know anything about Gordon?"

"I saw him quite a few times when he came here, but I know nothing about him personally."

"Listen, Rebecca, I feel like I am not getting the whole story about what's going on with Gordon and all this money that I have received from him."

"What is it that you need to know? And Lena, why do you have to know where the money came from? Honey, you should be glad that someone left you a such a large sum of money."

"So you know where the money came from?"

Rebecca placed her hand on her full hip. "I don't know anything about it, all I know is that you should be somewhere enjoying it."

"I think you know, Rebecca, what type of work does Marvin do?"

"Lena, I think it's time for you to go. Whatever my husband does it's none of your business. Tessa, can you please escort Miss Lena to the door and see her out."

"Please, Rebecca, I need to know."

"Goodbye, Lena." Without saying another word, Rebecca walked away with her floral flowing top waving behind her.

* * *

When I got home, I went into my office and looked up online the going prices for the houses in my neighborhood. I twisted up my lips at what I saw. Mr. Dobson had lied to me about the price of my house. The homes in this area were going for over three million dollars, some as high as ten million. With the size of my house, I knew I was in the higher range. I just couldn't figure out all the secrecy that was going on. *All these men were rich, but how did they become so wealthy?* I never really knew what type of work Gordon did. Most of the time, he didn't seem to be doing much work. He did mention something to me about the stock market, that he enjoyed investing. Being that I knew nothing about stocks or investing, nothing more was ever said about it.

The more I dug, the less information I got. It was like I was at a dead end. I had worked myself up so much about having all this money that I wasn't t able to sleep well. I would search online, trying to find out things about Gordon, Lonny, and Marvin; I came up with nothing. I even hired a few private investigators. They would begin their research, and within a few days, they would call me back, telling me that they were no longer interested in handling my case.

* * *

Unable to get any answers about Gordon, I made up my mind to focus on raising Elijah. Tracey, the boys, and I had been living in Hawaii for two years. Tracey was enrolled in the community college, taking classes to become a domestic violence counselor. She also volunteered at local schools, speaking to young children and teens about the importance of reporting the crime of domestic violence. She used to be ashamed to show her hand with the missing fingers and of the looks she would get from people looking at the scar on her face, but she turned that around to show just what can happen if you don't do something about it. Tracey had finally found a place where she was free, turning her negative into a positive.

The boys were in kindergarten. They were on the honor roll every month. At five years old, they were competing in surfing competitions and winning. Tracey and I were enjoying ever aspect of the boys' lives. We would attend school plays, participate in bake sales, and organize fundraisers for the PTA. Not wanting to be treated differently, I would donate to the school program anonymously. We had met a great group of people that we had fun socializing with. We also enjoyed our neighbors. I opened up my stand for tourists. I also hired a girl to run it.

She was a young, single mother, raising two children, who was grateful to have a job, one that allowed her to bring her children to work with her. She was a hard worker, keeping the shop in tip-top shape. Whenever I had a few hours to spare, I would take a seat in the shop selling some items.

I had taken a liking to photography. I had become a freelance photographer. Most of my work showed the beauty in the lives of the invisible people in our world. Doing photography had allowed me to meet some of the most amazing people, that most people don't even see as people. I have displayed my work in museums, art shows, and have even sold a few pieces. My next endeavor was to go to Paris to show the beauty that I see through the lens. I brought an enormous building for kids and teens to come and express their artistic abilities, in any form that they chose, which brings me great joy. I've purchased video cameras, still cameras, computers, all kinds of instruments, paints, and canvases. I even had a dark room installed.

We have arts and crafts, cooking classes, counseling classes, and a large dance studio. I also invited people from different islands to come and show their artistic work and abilities to the kids. Some nights, we would have a movie night outside of the building on a big screen that I purchased for the kids. We would set it up just like we were in a movie theater. It was all great fun. The kids would put on plays and talent shows. They all enjoyed the studio. Many of the kids that come to the recreation building have nowhere else to go. Some come because it was the only safe place they have, the only place they could get a hot meal and snacks, and others come just to release the pain that they hold on to. They all learn something about themselves, their value, and their self worth, something that I had never known growing up.

* * *

Most days are good days, but I have some that don't allow me to think about anything but the love of my life. Those are the days when it's hard for me to get out of bed to face the world. Even living in paradise can feel like living in misery. That's when I look deep into the eyes of my son to find the peace that I need and long for. To find the sunshine when there is no sun shining inside of me. My past sometimes crawls into bed with me. It lies next to me, wanting to keep me all to itself, for me to hold on to the memories that we once shared, wanting to stay with me, to relive those bad thoughts repeatedly in my mind. I have to fight it off of me so that I can breathe, so I can go on with determination.

A few times, I had contacted Kelly, Tracey's psychiatrist. When I contacted her, she was pleased that I reached out to her. Being that I no longer was living the South Bronx, she agreed to my terms, so we would do a few sessions over the phone. For me, I felt more comfortable doing them that way. I was not good at expressing myself about my past to people. I didn't have to see Kelly's reaction. In turn, see couldn't see mine. A few times, she would get quiet after hearing about some of the things I had endured at the hands of my mother. She had helped me, to the best of her ability, to understand about my childhood. I must admit that talking about my issues with Kelly had helped me tremendously. She had unlocked the truth; it was never about me, it was about my parents. They were toxic towards each other, allowing it to trickle down to me. Neither one of them knew how to love. Trying to mix their dysfunctional love together was like oil and water; it never meshed. Having me just added more to their dysfunction, leaving me dead and center in their war. Kelly's words had become conformation to me about my parents. It was good to know that someone understood.

* * *

I felt that my life was full of unanswered questions, that I may never receive the truth or get the answers. People that I know little about seem to have a lot of secrets. They hide behind their smiles and their riches. Even if they wanted me to fit into their cliques, I wouldn't. It wasn't who I really was. I was outside of the box and they knew it. They would invite me to their social gatherings, but if what I wore was something that didn't live up to their standards, or the way that I spoke made them feel uncomfortable, their invites would become far and few. I felt that they only dealt with me because I was rich. Maybe they felt obligated to the ties they had with Gordon. I really didn't know. They knew that if there were some type of charitable organizations that was dear to my heart, I would get involved, giving substantial donations. Those times, they would kiss up to me. Whatever I did wasn't for them, but for the greater good, for those that needed the funding. Even though Gordon was no longer alive, accepting me, I could feel that it gave them a feeling of loyalty to him.

My heart was too real for them. They couldn't understand how I wasn't willing to fit into the status quo, to live like rich people do. To hell with them. I had to raise my son grounded, to know who he was, not what we had. His start in this life began in a dirty alleyway, coming from the inside of my womb, landing on filthy a piece of cardboard. Elijah's beginnings were humble. I would let him know that, never letting him forget that he was a naive New Yorker, straight out of the South Bronx, whose first home was on the streets of the city, not living in the most beautiful place on earth.

Having this money had not changed me. The only thing that it did was give me the power to change a little part of the world, to make a difference in the lives of others. I will never let the girl inside of me that grew up in the South Bronx die. She has become my lifeline. Even through all of the pain she had to live through, she was a survivor, strong and fearless. She should have worn an "S" on her chest for all that she had been through. Even though people could not see it, she could fly, leaping tall building in a single bound. Even while having two parents that were her kryptonite, she still made it. She fought through poverty, homelessness, rapes, domestic violence, forced abortions neglect and too many pains to count. Was she super? You damn right she was.

* * *

It has taken me a while to embrace God, but when I started to read His word, I saw a lot of me in there, a lot of Jesus in me, too. His life wasn't easy. He's the King of Kings, and the Lord of Lords, yet He was born in a manger where they kept animals, He was laid in a trough where animal would feed. Just like the South Bronx, Jesus grew up in Nazareth, a place where people said no good thing could ever come from. People didn't like Him because He did not come to make the world like Him, but instead, to turn it upside down. He came to bring the truth to those who thought that they were right. He was a revolutionary. I never really saw myself in that light, but looking back over my life to where I am today, I was born to be that.

My life was hard on every level. Growing up in the ghetto was not just my life but my state of mind. I often asked myself what good could come from living in a situation that was bleak, dark, and over loaded with a lack of hope. Truth be told, my world was upside down. I had to fight to graduate from high school. I had to fight to eat. I had to fight to keep my son. I had to fight to live in my mother's house. I had to fight to stay alive. You just don't become a fighter overnight; you are born with it. It is inbred deep within your spirit, never leaving you.

Yet, through it all I had sprung forth like a flower amongst thorns.

* * *

Mrs. Parker had called me, informing me that my mother had passed away. She also told me that mother had been clean and sober for a while, and that the cancer in her body had run its course. My mother had someone contact Mrs. Parker, telling her that she wanted to see her. She wanted Mrs. Parker to tell me that she was sorry and that she loved Elijah and I. There was silence mixed with many emotions. When I heard the words come out of Mrs. Parker's mouth, that my mother had died, it didn't feel like I thought that it would. There was no marching band playing, no confetti falling from the sky, no cheers, no dancing, and no neon lights flashing, stating that my mother was dead. It didn't feel like the dark clouds had been rolled away from my life, allowing the bright sunshine to beam down on my face, signifying that all the diabolical, destructiveness of my mother had come to an end. What I did feel was remorse that she did not know me. My mother allowed herself to miss out on the blessing that God had given her in me. She never knew my favorite color, never knew my love for the arts, or my ability to write music. My mother let the hatred inside of her cloud her mind. It had cheated her out a life of knowing love, giving love, and being loved. The majority of her time on earth was a bulk of wasted years, hours, minutes, and seconds. I couldn't thank her for showing me how to live, but I could thank her for giving me life.

I chose not to attend my mother's funeral. There was nothing that I wanted to see or say. I had seen and heard enough in my lifetime at the hands of her. I didn't want to look at my mother, to have the old feelings rise up inside of me. All the memories, all the pain, and all the hurt. I wanted them to be buried with her. I had sent money to Mrs. Parker to send flowers to the funeral from Elijah and me. I told Mrs. Parker that, if there were any expenses that needed to be covered, I would handle it. Another chapter of my life had been closed. This one did not bring me any joy, or peace. It was just done.

* * *

Twenty-four years I had been living on this earth. Even at a young age, I had reached a pinnacle in my life. I had learned not take anything in life for granted. God has given me knowledge that keeps being dropped down on me everyday, like manna from heaven, never once ceasing to amaze me. I have learned that, with the absence of my earthy father, it closed the door for me to be able to connect with my heavenly Father. How could I know His love if my own father rejected me? The enemy blinded me, causing me to seek out men that never loved me, nor had my best interest at heart. God revealed to me that He had always been my Father and my Mother. He was just waiting on me to open up my heart to let Him come in and heal me everywhere I was broken. For that, I am truly thankful to Him. Although Gordon is gone, I still love him. But I had to come to grips with the fact that even he was not totally honest with me. I had tried to receive a love, a peace, and a comfort from each of those men that only God could fully give me. I didn't ask for this life, but it was mine. I had to learn to accept it for what it was and move on the best way that I could. I had to release the poison of my mother and father from my life. I had to let go of the parents that I thought they should have been. Knowing that I would never have that, I opened up my hands, letting go of all my anger, pain, rejection, and disappointment. I let them go, like freeing a dove from my grip, watching it fly away until it could no longer be seen any more.

* * *

I sat on a lounge chair, enjoying the sounds of the crashing waves. I took a sip of ice cold water with a splash of lemon, while watching my son Elijah run past me. His small feet lifting tiny piles of white sand up behind them. He was free, running like the world has no boundaries, like he could not be stopped. He knew no beginning and no end. This is how I wanted him to view the world. Nothing in front and nothing behind could stop him from being all that he has been created to be. Never wanting his life to be one dimensional, but to be filled, multifaceted. The world was his oyster, ready for the taking. Elijah was not defined as Gordon's son or my son, but he was God's child, and he was destined to become our legacy.